Aja,

Follow the
dreams of your heart,
but always listen to
the wisdom of the
old ones.

love,
Aunt Carla
12/92

THE
BRIDGES
OF
SUMMER

THE
BRIDGES
OF
SUMMER

Brenda Seabrooke

COBBLEHILL BOOKS/DUTTON

New York

Library of Congress Cataloging-in-Publication Data
Seabrooke, Brenda.
The bridges of summer / Brenda Seabrooke.
p.   cm.
Summary: When she reluctantly comes to stay on a small South Carolina
island, fourteen-year-old Zarah gradually accepts her grandmother's
Gullah traditions and different way of life.
ISBN 0-525-65094-6
[1. Grandmothers—Fiction.   2. Islands—Fiction   3. South
Carolina—Fiction.   4. Afro-American—Fiction.]
PZ7.S4376Br   1992   [Fic]—dc20   92-11642   CIP   AC

Published in the United States by Cobblehill Books,
an affiliate of Dutton Children's Books,
a division of Penguin Books USA Inc.,
375 Hudson Street, New York, New York 10014
Designed by Joy Taylor
Printed in the United States of America
First Edition   10 9 8 7 6 5 4 3 2 1

Author's Note

DOMINGO, Saylor, and Barnett islands exist only in the author's mind, but they are based on Edisto, Hilton Head, and Daufuskie, South Carolina, and the Georgia islands, Ossabaw, Cumberland, Jekyll, and Saint Simons, and the Waccamaw and Cape Fear river areas of North Carolina. Even today with extensive development on some of them, the islands are wild and haunting and cast a seductive spell.

During the Civil War, Union troops liberated the South Carolina islands. The plantation owners fled and the former-slaves were allowed to own land for the first time. Those who worked hard and paid their taxes as Quanamina's family did held onto the land and passed it down to their descendants who still own it.

These descendants were known as Gullah, a word which is probably a corruption of Angola where many of the slave ancestors came from. The origin of Gullah is in dispute by linguists and historians.

In *The Bridges of Summer,* I have not attempted to reproduced the Gullah language, only to try to express the musical quality and flavor of the island speech.

This one is for Kerria

.

Remember the bridges that carry you over.

—GULLAH PROVERB

THE
BRIDGES
OF
SUMMER

Prologue

~~~~~~~~

I WAS fourteen when my mother sent me to visit my father's mother for the first time, sent me off to a black magic place. "It will only be for a little while," she said, giving me one of her cat looks.

I didn't want to go with her. Hanging around clubs in the Midwest wasn't my idea of a good summer, but neither was going to South Carolina. She was so excited running around fixing her costumes, getting her hair cut. "This is my big chance, Baby."

We left in the middle of the night, riding in Johnny's big maroon Cadillac, with "Johnny and the Maroons" stencilled on the door. New York looked gray and empty as we drove through the tunnel to New Jersey, but it was where my life was.

In Philadelphia they dropped me off at the station. Ila came in with me to buy my ticket. She gave me a quick hug.

"Wish me luck, Baby," and she was gone, west to Pittsburgh, only the ghost of her spicy perfume to mark where she had been.

The bus was late. I had to wait forty-five minutes to go to Charleston, to a place beyond Charleston, beyond this century, to a place I could not have imagined before that summer.

ONE

~~~~~

YONDER lies Domingo Island," the bus driver told Zarah as he handed down her biggest suitcase.

"Where?" Zarah squinted in the sunlight, still strong in late afternoon. Stretching as far as she could see were marshes of tall grass and dark growths of trees with the feathered heads of palm trees sticking up here and there like shaggy-headed animals surprised in their grazing. Close to the horizon three white birds coasted on unseen air currents. Zarah couldn't see water anywhere.

You couldn't have an island without water. Everybody knew that. Water was what made an island an island.

Zarah looked back at the driver. He was still standing on the top step, folding a stick of gum. He put it in his mouth and tossed the balled paper into the road where it rolled into a pothole.

"I don't see any island," Zarah said.

The driver looked annoyed. He chewed his gum a few

times before answering. "It's there, all right. You just follow this road till you come to a camel bridge and after you get over that, you're on Saylor's Island. Domingo is over the next bridge, if you can call it that." He pointed down the road. "Right down there," he said again.

What did he mean if you can call it that? A bridge was a bridge or it wasn't. It couldn't be anything else. The driver was already behind the wheel before she could ask what a camel bridge was.

"OK, thanks," she said. The door closed with a hiss. The green and white bus rattled off, "Low Country Rover" in orange letters on the side. It disappeared around a curve, leaving her alone with her luggage on the side of the road.

More like "No Country Rover," she thought. The only sign that humans had ever been here was the road, a two-lane strip of concrete, broken and pitted with weeds growing through it that led off through the chin-high grass. No island. No people. Zarah sighed. She couldn't stay here. She shouldered her smaller bag, picked up her Bloomingdale's shopping bag and started off down the road, pulling her large suitcase in the direction the driver had pointed.

The suitcase was an old one of Londra's, a friend of her mother's, and was designed to roll on little wheels through airports or along city pavements. It wasn't made for cracked, rotting pavement. The suitcase bumped along behind Zarah, bounced out of holes and overturned. The wheels caught on things and stuck, jerking Zarah off-balance so that once she fell on top of her Bloomingdale's bag. She hoped nothing had broken.

She got up, kicked the suitcase, then kicked the pavement. She kicked too hard and hurt her toe. Sandals weren't made for kicking. Zarah was fourteen and didn't normally kick things anymore except as a last resort. You couldn't get even with an inanimate object. But Ila had sent her to the end of the world and she had to take it out on something.

~~~~~~~

IT WILL only be for a little while," her mother had said. "Just till I can get things together. Besides it will be good for you to get to know your grandmother."

Zarah didn't think much of going off to visit somebody she didn't know, even if it was her father's mother.

"You met her once," Ila went on, "when you were little."

"I didn't. I would've remembered." Anybody would remember a grandmother who owned an island, a whole island. But that could be another of Ila's stories. She could make the truth do aerobics when she wanted to, bending and stretching it. Ila never wanted to talk about her past, growing up on Mosquito Point, in South Carolina, near Charleston where her family was so poor they had to carry water from a well and use an outhouse for a bathroom. Ila liked to pretend she had always lived in New York. But sometimes she let things slip. "How little?" Zarah asked.

"When you were little. About six." Her mother had looked away.

"Six years? I definitely would've remembered."

"Oh, you were probably more like six months."

"Nobody remembers anything when they are six months."

"That's not true. I remember quite clearly a pot of red geraniums when I was a baby. The cat used to sleep under them on the porch. It was a black cat. It was the only time we had a porch. That's how I know I was a baby. Because of the porch." Ila closed her eyes. "They used to let me sleep on the porch when it was hot. If I cried, they rocked me. Then my daddy came and we moved to the North. We didn't ever have a porch after I was a baby." Ila hugged her arms and rocked, humming a lullaby.

Zarah had watched in fascination. Then she broke the spell. "You were ten years old when you moved north. Londra told me."

Her mother tossed her head. Her curls were wild black clouds before a storm. Ivory bells in her ears tinkled. "Londra wasn't there."

Zarah seized the moment. "I don't want to go down there and miss my ballet classes. I'll get behind. Why can't I stay with Londra?"

"Londra is going to California. You know that. She may be gone all summer. It won't be for long, Baby. I'm tired of little, nothing jobs. Your daddy's insurance money and Social Security won't last forever. This is my big chance."

Zarah didn't call singing with Johnny and the Maroons at small clubs in the Midwest a big chance. Still it was the best chance Ila'd ever had. Londra had brought over the big suitcase with a shoulder bag inside it. It was the biggest suitcase Zarah had ever seen. You could pack a mattress in it if you could get it folded. "I don't need it," she'd protested. "I don't need to take that much. I'm not going to be there that long."

Londra had given Ila a look, then said, "It's always better to take more. You never know what you'll need."

"You better take a lot of stuff," Ila had said. "It's like a foreign country down there. You don't know what you might need and there aren't any stores."

"Why is it like a foreign country?" Zarah asked.

"It's just different. You'll see. They even speak another language."

"What language?"

"Gullah."

"I never heard of a language called Gullah. What's Gullah?"

But her mother had gone into the kitchen singing,

> "De slave dey come from Africa
> on boats with wings
> and jaws of death
> crossing de water fa."

"Gullah is slave talk," Londra had said.

~~~~~~~~

A CLOUD of gnats hovered in front of Zarah's face. They hung in the air just above her nose so that she had to look through them like a gray curtain until they darted at her eyes. Zarah blew up at them. They scattered briefly, then returned. She picked a handful of long, reedy weeds growing in a pothole and shook them in front of her as she walked.

"Stupid. This is stupid." She spoke out loud. "Stupid!" she shouted.

There was a splash somewhere in the grass to her left. On her right a huge blue-gray bird rose on powerful wings and flew off to find a quieter marsh. Zarah walked a bit more warily. She'd thought herself all alone on the road. Now she knew there were things around her.

The late afternoon sun burned into the road. The air was like warm glue. Soon Zarah's orange rayon dress stuck to her in uncomfortable places and the straps of her sandals felt like hot wires cutting into her swelling feet. She wished she could take the sandals off but the pavement would be too hot to walk on with bare feet. She could feel it through the thin soles of the sandals that had been so chic in New York. She didn't want to take time to stop and dig through her suitcases for sneakers. It would be dark soon and there were no street-lights out here.

The sun seemed to be sinking of its own weight as it burned a fiery hole in the sky on her left. Zarah wondered how long it would take to get to the island. Then she wondered if the road really went there. She only had the bus driver's word. Maybe he didn't know for sure. Maybe he was wrong.

The camel bridge looked like a camel. It went straight up in a hump without any gradual rise and came down on the other side of the river. CULEBRA RIVER the sign said. Zarah shivered despite the heat. What a horrible name. In Spanish it meant snake. It looked like a snake, too, dark and oily. There was no telling what was in that dark water.

She had to carry the big suitcase over the bridge. It was too steep for her to pull the suitcase up one side and control it going down on the other side. Zarah made two trips over the bridge. Things were moving in the dirty mud alongside the water. Ugly, crablike things. They made clicking sounds.

A wooden sign on the other side of the bridge said SAY-LOR'S ISLAND, SOUTH CAROLINA. Zarah sat down on the big suitcase and rummaged in her purse until she found the map Ila had drawn for her.

Ila had said, "I've only been there twice and that was a long time before you were born. But it won't be changed any. The only way those places change is for a development company to buy it all up. That won't happen long as the Saylor family is still breathing. And your grandmother."

So maybe her grandmother did own the island. But Zarah knew she had never met her grandmother before, never been to South Carolina. Ila just didn't want Zarah to think that she was being sent to the end of the world to a grandmother she didn't even know.

"After you cross the bridge," Ila had said, "you go left. The paved road to the right goes to the Saylors' house and landing. You take the shell road till you come to a bridge over a little marshy creek. Cross that and you're on Domingo Island. At the end of the road is your grandmother's house. You can't miss it. Nobody else lives there."

Zarah put the map in her pocket and stood up. It was getting darker. She looked at her watches. She wore three from her collection on her right wrist. The red one with a polka dot band set on Eastern Standard Time said 8:44. The Egyptian one set on Egyptian time said 2:42. The plastic palm tree with the watch face set in a coconut hanging from it gave California time and it said 5:48.

Two of them were wrong. Or maybe all three but whatever time it was, Zarah knew it was getting late. She pulled the big suitcase but it balked on the road graveled with oyster shells and fell over its front in a somersault. Zarah discovered that it rolled better if she kept it in the ruts where the shells had been crushed almost to a powder. But even then an occasional large piece stuck in the wheels and she had to stop and pull it out.

The sun disappeared behind her, leaving a yellowish light that you didn't get in New York City or any civilized place Zarah had ever been in. She could still see the river with its black water and black mud banks but it was not a sight that made her feel better about her situation, stuck in the middle of a swamp on an island in the middle of nowhere. The river looked like the kind that could slither out of its banks and get you.

The shell road ended at another bridge. It wasn't a camel bridge, just a bunch of rickety boards laid over more black water that wasn't as wide as the river. Now she knew why the bus driver had said if you can call it a bridge. Zarah tested the first board with her toe. It seemed sturdy enough. She pulled the suitcase onto it. The boards sagged and shook on their pilings as she crept across them. If she ever got on the island, she knew she could never leave if she had to go back across that awful bridge.

The light was almost gone now. Zarah had no idea how far down the road her grandmother's house was. She seemed to have been walking all day. She had walked for miles, probably about ten at least. Ila must have forgotten how far it was. Or maybe she thought the bus went all the way to the island. Zarah wished she had a flashlight. She could see the white gleam of the shell track. That wasn't the problem. It was the black curtain of bushes and vines on each side of her that she needed light for. And for the things in the bushes, things with teeth and claws. And fangs.

There were sounds in the blackness. Fluttering, slithering (she remembered the river and the creek), gulping, gurgling, swishing, clicking, groaning, all horrible sounds when you didn't know what made them. Zarah jumped at a screech that ripped the darkness. Her eyes were fixed on the road. She couldn't decide whether to walk quietly so whatever creatures abroad wouldn't hear her or to stamp and make a lot of noise to scare them away.

She decided noise would be the best defense. She brought her feet down with force, grinding from side to side before she picked them up again. And she sang. "I'm a purple plumed baby in a picked chicken world."

She sang Ila's songs. In between she whistled. She was just finishing "A pair of aces ain't enough when your baby's gone and left," when she saw a pale glow ahead. Grandmother's house at last.

Zarah started to run toward the light, to safety. The big suitcase seesawed crazily behind her. The Bloomingdale's bag and shoulder bag bounced under her arm.

A voice came out of the light. "Who that ouchander? Speak up. I got this gun point at you gullet."

TWO

~~~~

ZARAH FROZE. She couldn't see the house. It was a window-shaped blur of light in the blackness of the night. Could she have come to the wrong house? The wrong island? There was only one way to find out.

She took a deep breath. "I'm looking for Quanamina Brown of Domingo Island. Is this her house?"

"Maybe is, maybe ain't."

Zarah took a step toward the light.

"Don't come any closer. This gun aim right at you gullet. Get away from here now before it go off."

Zarah considered running. That was what the voice wanted her to do. But it might shoot her in the back. And if she did run, where would she run to? She could see nothing but darkness. She crouched behind her suitcase. Broken shells cut into her knees but there was no time to worry about them now.

"I'm looking for Quanamina Brown. Is this where she lives?"

"Who want to know?"

"Me. Princess Zarah Brown. I'm her granddaughter."

"Quanamina don't have no granddaughter name Princess Zarah."

"Yes, she does. She knows me as Sarah Jane."

"Sarah Jane? That you?"

The light brightened. Zarah could see now it was a window behind a screened porch. She heard the scrape of a door opening, the whine of a screen door.

"Come on in here, child."

Zarah stood up. Bits of shell stuck in her knees. She picked up her bags and started toward the light, praying that it wasn't some kind of trick and she wasn't going to get her head blown off.

"Hurry, child. This house get full up with skeeters."

"What?"

Quanamina pointed at a cloud of mosquitoes whining around Zarah's head.

"Oh. Mosquitoes."

Zarah's legs felt weak but she walked faster. The figure in the doorway took on its own shape as she neared. What she had seen as a giant hulk was only one old woman with a small boy clinging like a shadow to the back of her skirt.

"I'm Quanamina," the woman said when Zarah was inside. "He Loomis." The boy ducked behind Quanamina so fast that Zarah only had an impression of enormous eyes. What was the matter with the kid? Hadn't he ever seen a girl before?

Zarah didn't know what she had expected in her grandmother. But she hadn't expected her to pick up the kerosene lamp and hold it close to Zarah while she looked her up and down.

"Guess you real enough," she said when she got to Zarah's shell-decorated knees. "Sit you down." She almost pushed Zarah into a sagging, overstuffed green chair.

She made Zarah hold the lamp while she picked the shell bits out of her knees. The left one was bleeding. Quanamina brought a bowl of water from another room and washed both knees. Then she smeared some smelly stuff on them that stung worse than the shell bits had.

"You hungry?"

"Yes, please."

The old woman grunted something that sounded like, "Least you got manners."

She went into another room. The boy Loomis followed. Zarah looked around. The room was crowded with things which made it seem smaller than it was, two sagging couches, four chairs, several tables of polished dark wood. The walls were hung with pictures and shelves but Zarah couldn't see what was on them in the lamplight. She made out a few of the pictures. They appeared to be religious scenes and at least two were of Jesus.

Quanamina came back, the boy still behind her. She put a tray which held a plate, a spoon, a cloth napkin ironed as smooth as satin, and a glass of water on the table beside Zarah. She sat down on the blue sofa. It sagged further with her weight. Loomis went behind her. For a minute Zarah thought she and her grandmother were floating on two billowing waves, one blue and the other green, and that Loomis had ducked under the blue one. She swallowed her giggle. It wouldn't be polite.

The plate held slimy green stuff, a big piece of corn bread, and an orange potato-looking thing. "What is it?"

"Where you been, child, you don't know greens and sweet potato and corn bread?"

Zarah opened her mouth to say where people eat real food. She couldn't eat that, didn't they have yogurt or a cheeseburger or a salad, the kind of food she was used to? Ila and Londra were always on diets and Zarah ate what they did. Instead, she took a bite and found to her surprise that the bitterness of the greens was just right when eaten with corn bread smeared with sweet potato. Loomis gnawed on a piece of the corn bread. He sounded like a little squirrel behind the chair.

Quanamina didn't talk until Zarah had finished and she had taken the tray away. Then she sat down in the big stuffed brown rocker. The lamp was beside her on a table with a Bible, glasses, a small gold vase of marigolds, scissors, threads, a bristling pincushion, a magnifying glass, an ashtray decorated with shells, another made of bright blue glass, and small figurines of ladies in long pastel dresses. The table and the room were too full of things. Zarah liked empty spaces where she could move, do an *arabesque*, if she wanted to. She felt hot and claustrophobic in all this clutter.

"Now tell me how you appear out of the dark in front of my house," her grandmother said.

"Didn't my mother write to you? She said she had."

Quanamina was quiet for a minute. Then she opened a carved wooden box on the table beside her and took out a letter. It looked worn, as though it had been taken out of its envelope many times. "This the one?"

It was Ila's pointed script in purple ink on pale mauve

paper. Zarah would recognize it anywhere, even across a room. "Yes. That's Ila's letter. Didn't you read it?"

Quanamina didn't answer. She put the letter back in the box and waited. After a minute Zarah explained about Ila and the job with the band. When she finished Quanamina was silent for so long that Zarah thought she had gone to sleep. She stole a look. Her grandmother's eyes were open. A breeze blew in the front window, lifting the corner of the white cloth on the little table, ruffling her grandmother's skirt, cooling Zarah's knees.

"You going back?" Quanamina asked.

"Of course I am. I didn't come here to live."

"Buy you a ticket back?"

"No. They bought me a ticket here. I rode with the band as far as Philadelphia. Ila didn't have enough for a round trip. She's going to send it to me."

The old woman rocked awhile. The rocker creaked rhythmically. The sound irritated Zarah.

"She will." Zarah's voice came out louder than she intended in the silence. Loomis jumped back. Why didn't her grandmother believe her?

"Ila May always was a going-to girl," Quanamina said.

Zarah peered through the lamplight. It was different from the lighting she was used to, heavier somehow and light and dark at the same time. You couldn't see people as well but you could feel things stronger. Zarah thought she could feel her grandmother's disapproval of Ila. And of Zarah.

Zarah jumped up. "Ila sent you a present. I almost forgot." She tore through her bag and pulled out a pale orchid peignoir. It was one of Londra's. Somebody had given it to her but she'd never worn it. "Lavender is for old ladies," she'd said. "Take it to your grandmother." Zarah held it out but Quanamina didn't take it.

"What I want with something like that? That for fancy lady."

But her hand reached out to stroke the sheer fabric. "It sure soft." Loomis touched it with a shy finger.

"Look at them ruffle round the neck."

"It's got satin ribbons." Zarah laid the peignoir across her grandmother's lap. Quanamina smoothed the silky folds. Her arms were heavy, her hands gnarly with veins sticking up. They looked like the roots Zarah had tripped over in the dark.

"What a fat old woman want with something like this," she muttered. "Can't wear it to church. Can't wear it no-where."

"You can wear it here," Zarah said. "Wear it here for yourself."

"Child, you don't have to sell nothing. Not to me," she added softly. Then she smiled and the folds in her face seemed to melt until her face for an instant in the dark-light glow from the lamp looked young. "Fold it up nice for me and put it in the trunk and sprinkle some of that in it." She pointed to a can on a shelf over the trunk in the corner.

Loomis had crept from behind Quanamina's chair to sit on a stool beside her. He jumped up. "I'll get it," he said. He climbed on the trunk and stretched for the can but he was too short. His fingers only grazed the bottom of the can but in his eagerness he pushed at it too hard. The can tipped over and its lid flew off, spilling the contents over Loomis and onto the floor.

Loomis stood on the trunk like a stricken little boy statue, his eyes darting from Zarah to Quanamina, waiting for one of them to react so he could cry.

"Look, some of the yarbs fell on it already," Quanamina said. "Hop down, Loomis, and help Sarah Jane get it up."

A tingly smell, both sweet and sharp, rose from the floor. Zarah scooped up what looked like tiny flowers, seeds, and rose petals. She threw them over the peignoir and laid it in the trunk on top of something white. The trunk smelled the same, only stronger from being closed.

Loomis was still on the floor picking up the herbs, too busy to cry. Zarah spied a broom behind the door. She picked it up to sweep the pieces too small to pick up but Quanamina stopped her.

"Be plenty time tomorrow for that."

"It won't take but a minute," Zarah said, still sweeping.

"No!" Her grandmother's voice was sharp and authoritative. "No," she said again in a quieter voice. "It be bad luck sweep after dark."

Zarah stared at her. What did Quanamina mean, bad luck? She had used a broom plenty of times after dark.

Quanamina's eyes held Zarah's. "No," she repeated. "This don't be New York. This be Gullah country."

"What's that?" Ila had never explained about Gullah. "Slave talk" Londra had said. But there were no slaves now and hadn't been for over a hundred years.

"Place where Gullah people live. I be Gullah. You Gullah, too."

No, she was a New Yorker. This place, this weird island was nothing to do with her. Zarah replaced the broom. She felt tired and sleepy. Where would she sleep? She turned to ask.

Quanamina pulled herself up out of the chair. She took

Zarah to a small bedroom off a hall. An owl called out in the night. Loomis looked scared. "That a hu hu?" he asked.

"No, only a bidi bidi."

"Oh." He seemed relieved. But when he went into another bedroom off the hall, Quanamina turned the pockets of her apron inside out and tied a knot in the sheet on Zarah's bed. "You be safe now," she said.

THREE

~~~~~~~

THE PILLOW felt wet to Zarah's cheek, as though she had cried into it during the night. She touched her face. Her eyes were dry. The bed felt moist, too. The top sheet was twisted into a damp snake that twined around her legs. She kicked her legs free and got up.

Her clothes hung on the chair where she had dropped them the night before. Her suitcase lay open on the floor. Zarah stood on a faded blue rag rug and dug around until she found a pair of cerise shorts, a green T-shirt, and purple sneakers. She kicked the gold sandals under the bed. They had blistered her feet for the last time. She winced as she pulled a pair of white socks over the blisters, then the sneakers. She wasn't going barefoot around here. She'd read about worms and things in the South.

Zarah straightened the sheets. Had she sweated that much during the night? She pulled a patchwork quilt up off the floor where it had fallen. It felt damp, too, and she hadn't touched it. Zarah smoothed the red and blue pinwheels of the quilt pattern and plumped the pillow. She set it against the dark carved headboard. The bed looked as though it hadn't been slept in.

This room was as bare as the other room had been cluttered. Besides the bed, a nightstand, a dresser, a chifforobe, and a straight-legged chair were the only pieces of furniture. She looked in the mirror. Her hair was starting to frizz the way it always did in high humidity. That must be what made the bed feel wet. She couldn't believe that humidity could do that to sheets.

Zarah went over to the window. She leaned on the sill and looked out. The kid Zoomis or Loomis was out there scratching the bare ground with a broom made of twigs bound together.

"What are you doing?"

He looked up, saw her, and ducked around the side of the house. She wondered if there was something wrong with him. Why was he sweeping the dirt? Maybe it was some kind of busy work.

Quanamina wasn't in the living room or on the front porch. Zarah was reluctant to enter her bedroom. She listened for a minute but there was only silence behind the closed door. She went to the kitchen. Her grandmother wasn't there either.

Zarah opened a cabinet and found dishes in an assortment of patterns. She opened another cabinet and found a jar of instant coffee and in another a pot. But she couldn't find water. There was no sink, no faucet, no water. She turned a knob on the stove and watched it awhile. The coil stayed cool.

Then she noticed the quiet. The refrigerator at home hummed. This one didn't. She could hear the faint swishing sound of Loomis's sweeping, the clucking of chickens, bird-calls, the distant sound of a motor. But the refrigerator stayed silent. Zarah opened it. The air that met her face was as warm as the air in the room. The shelves were crowded with staples—flour, sugar, rice, cornmeal—things that mice would eat.

Zarah closed the door. Quanamina didn't have electricity or running water. That would mean no bathroom either. She hadn't been since she'd stopped behind a bush when she first came on the island. She became aware of discomfort but it was pushed aside by another feeling that was even worse. What was she going to do in this place with that strange old woman who didn't seem to like her and that weird little boy?

She should have got a summer job, gone to summer school, broken her leg, anything to keep from coming to this place. This island was not only isolated from the rest of the world in distance but also in time. It was like being in another century. Zarah wasn't used to quiet. It got on her nerves. She missed the sounds of city traffic, subways and vendors, the blaring horns, screeching tires.

The screen door creaked behind her. Zarah spun around.

"You hungry for breakfast?" Quanamina asked. She was carrying a platter of fried eggs and biscuits and a pitcher of milk. She set them on the white-painted table.

"Loomis," she called out the door. "Get some plates out the dresser," she said to Zarah.

Zarah started to say that she didn't eat eggs but instead she said OK and got three flowered plates out of the cabinet. She would eat one egg to be polite and to fill her stomach.

Loomis propped his broom against the side of the house and sidled into the kitchen. Quanamina gave him a stern look. "Hand," she said.

He went out on the back porch. Zarah heard an energetic squeaking, then the gush of water.

"What was that?"

"Pump," Quanamina said as she took a pitcher of syrup out of the refrigerator.

"Why don't you have electricity? You must have had it in the past."

"Did. Storm knocked down the line. I owed on my bill. Power company say they won't put the line back."

"If you couldn't pay your bills, how could you afford the stove and refrigerator?"

"My husband get them for me."

"But how do you cook?"

"Out in the shed."

Loomis came back and spread his hands for Quanamina to see. He sat down on a stool at the table without looking at Zarah. Then she and her grandmother sat down. Zarah looked at the plates of food. The eggs bulged in the center like great popping yellow eyes. There was also a pile of fried slabs of something white with streaks of brown in it.

"Help yourself," Quanamina said.

Zarah took an egg without looking at its center. "What's that?" Her fork hovered over the pile.

"Side meat."

Loomis giggled.

Zarah ate it all without looking at it. She finished with a biscuit mopped in the strong-tasting syrup. Her stomach felt heavy. It was accustomed to yogurt or cereal first thing in the morning.

"Where is the bathroom?" she asked, dreading the answer.

"Ouchonder."

"Where?" Zarah couldn't understand some of her grandmother's words.

"Ouchander. Loomis show you."

He slid out of his chair. Zarah followed him across the hard-packed sandy yard striped with lines from his broom. They passed a shed with a stove where Quanamina must have cooked the breakfast. She could still feel the heat. Zarah couldn't imagine living without electricity. Then Loomis pointed to a building that could only be an outhouse.

She opened the door and went in. The walls didn't go all the way to the ceiling so there was light. But what would she do at night? Zarah shuddered.

Loomis was scratching away with the twig broom when she came out. "Why does he do that?" she asked her grandmother back in the house.

"So we can tell if snake come in the house."

"Snake?" Zarah felt her skin crawl.

"Snake leave tracks if they crawl over broom lines. Then we see where they go and kill 'em."

So Loomis wasn't crazy.

"What dress you have for church?" Quanamina asked.

Zarah showed her the purple Charmeuse, the red and black striped silk, and the green satin, dresses that Londra had discarded. Quanamina shook her head. "Them won't do for church. I'll make one for you." She rummaged in the drawer of a treadle sewing machine and pulled out a yellow measuring tape and a pattern that had been folded many times. She measured Zarah's waist.

"How old you now?"

"Fourteen."

"You big for fourteen. Tall like you daddy."

Zarah was pleased. "I look like him, too."

"You look like Ila May," Quanamina said.

"I don't. I do not look like her." Zarah didn't want to look like her mother or be like her, never following through on things or, when she did, stupid things like going on tour with Johnny and the Maroons.

When Quanamina finished measuring, Zarah went outside. She stared at the woods around her. They were dark and thick and menacing except where the sun broke through. There was nowhere for her to go. She was stuck for however long Ila left her here, stuck with her strange grandmother and Loomis.

Loomis had already erased their footsteps to the outhouse. He jumped behind it when he saw Zarah, then peered around the corner. She frowned and went around the house to the front. Every time that kid saw her he jumped. It was making her nervous, as Ila would say.

Behind her she could hear him busily scratching out her footprints. Didn't he ever stop? Zarah walked down the shell track she had followed the night before until she was out of sight of the house. She found a stick and took off her right sneaker and sock. She put the sneaker back on her bare foot and tied the sock to the stick. She would give Loomis something to erase.

When he had swept her tracks away and returned to the back of the house, Zarah slipped to the front and made a snakelike track with the sock. She made it go from the edge of the woods all the way to the side of the front porch. Then she untied her sock and scratched out her footprints with the stick. Back on the shell track, she put her sock on again and walked to the house. She sat down on a sagging glider on the front porch and waited.

In a minute Loomis was there scratching her footprints out. Then he discovered the snake track. "Mina! Mina!" he yelled.

"What is it?"

"Snakey! Snakey!"

Quanamina came around the side of the house and looked at the tracks. Then she looked over at Zarah on the porch and shook her head slowly. "That not snake," she said.

"It conjure?"

"No. Just a worm."

Quanamina came up on the porch. Zarah didn't dare look up. She could feel Quanamina's eyes on her.

"He only five," she said. Then she went in the house. Zarah heard the treadle of the sewing machine going up and down, clickety clack, clickety clack.

Zarah sat back on the glider to think. How did Quanamina know it wasn't a real snake?

FOUR

~~~~

ZARAH punched the buttons on her Walkman. The batteries were still dead. They had run out when she was on the bus somewhere in North Carolina. The Walkman might as well be a stick of wood for all the good it was doing her. She shoved it under her chair.

"Isn't there a place to buy batteries around here?" she asked.

Quanamina was basting collar pieces she had cut from white fabric she'd taken out of the trunk. She bit off the thread before answering. "Not on Domingo. Store on Barnett maybe sell battery. I don't know." She squinted through the glasses that slid down her nose. "You see to thread this needle for me?" She held the spool of white thread and needle out to Zarah.

Zarah threaded the needle. She had been sewing the elastic on her ballet shoes since she was eight. She handed the needle back to her grandmother who grunted her thanks.

Quanamina still seemed to disapprove of Zarah. But she hadn't mentioned the snake again. Loomis was on the floor beside Quanamina's chair playing with scraps of the white fabric. He was tying the scraps into a crazy rope.

They were on the back porch where Quanamina said the light was better. It wasn't screened like the front porch but there didn't seem to be any mosquitoes in the early afternoon. Zarah leaned back in her chair. The rocker hit the edge of her Walkman with a loud thump. The chicken in the yard squawked and leaped in the air. Its eyes darted around the broomswept yard, then it went back to its pecking. It was the craziest chicken Zarah had ever seen. It looked like it had stuck its beak in an electric socket. Its white feathers were long, flopping around its face and body more like hair than feathers. All the other ordinary chickens were kept in a pen behind the outhouse.

"What kind of chicken is that?"

"Frizzle chicken."

"I never heard of a frizzle chicken. Why isn't it penned up with the others?"

"Frizzle chicken find conjure bag."

That word again. "Conjure bag?"

"Somebody don't like you. Somebody want what you got, they put conjure bag under step, around house. Bad thing happen. Frizzle chicken find conjure bag, him feather fall out."

"What do you do about it?"

"See conjure man."

Zarah couldn't believe what she was hearing. This was still America even though it was South Carolina. Quanamina seemed to be in Africa or the Caribbean. "And he takes off the spell?"

" 'Pend. All kind of spell."

"Have you ever had a conjure on you?"

"Some mens wants something I got," Quanamina whispered.

Zarah couldn't believe that. What could Quanamina have that anybody would want? "And you think these men might put a conjure on you?"

But Quanamina didn't want to talk about spells. She jerked her head in the direction of Loomis. "Little pitcher got big ears," she said. "He afraid of conjure."

"I think I'll go explore the island," Zarah said. "Where does that go?" She pointed to a path beyond the cooking shed.

"To the ocean."

Quanamina didn't waste words, Zarah thought. Every path on this island must go to the ocean eventually or indirectly through the marsh or the river. She started down the track, putting each foot down with caution.

After a few feet the track curved. Zarah turned and looked back at the house. Quanamina and Loomis hadn't moved. She was still sewing and he was still tying up scraps. His twig broom and several cane poles were propped beside the back door. A wooden paddle hung on two nails over the door and a fishnet and baskets of various sizes hung from the wall. The house was really almost a shack. The wood had been painted white sometime, a long time ago but now it was weathered to a grayish color that blended into the sandy clearing, Zarah thought. But the boards framing the windows and doors had been freshly painted a bright blue. Why bother to paint the trim if you weren't going to paint the whole house? Why not let all of the house weather the same color? Zarah shrugged and turned back to the path through the jungly woods. Another island mystery.

As she went deeper, the whine of insects, the heat, thick, prickling, staccato, cloying, enveloped her. Gray moss like old, torn veils hung from the trees sometimes all the way to the ground, brushing her face as she passed underneath. Palmlike bushes with spiky fronds bristled close to the path, catching Zarah's elbow with a vicious jab. Vines clambered up tree trunks, twined around their limbs, and snaked across the path.

Everything looked snakey to Zarah. She wondered how you could even see a snake in this jungle. She supposed she would hear a rattlesnake.

Zarah's heart leaped at a nearby clicking sound. But it was only an insect. Then she jumped at a stick across the path. It was brown and thick like a snake. Zarah picked it up. It would make a good walking stick. She used it to beat the ground in front of her before each step.

She tried not to see snakes everywhere she looked. A butterfly with wings of sunlight landed on a bright orange flower and sipped its nectar. It looked harmless but the butterflies on Domingo probably had fangs.

Zarah heard the ocean before she saw it. She suddenly burst out of the jungle over a low dune onto a wide white beach so bright after the dark woods that she had to blink against the dazzling light. The beach looked just like a travel poster with palm trees along the edge of the sand. Zarah stared in amazement. Her grandmother lived in a pathetic house without electricity and running water and owned this gorgeous beach? It didn't make sense to her.

She took off her sneakers and socks and ran into the water. The waves lapped her ankles. The salt burned her blisters but it was probably good for them, she reasoned. She waded in the shallows, cooling her feet and legs up to her knees. She found a shell, fluted and spotted on its back, inside the palest pink. Zarah put it into her pocket.

She sat on a fallen palm trunk and watched the waves awhile. They had a rhythm. Zarah found herself keeping time to them. She stood up and held onto the raised palm roots. They were a little higher than a dancer's *barre* but she could make do. Zarah held onto the roots and did a *demi-plié*. Yes! It would work. She would have to stretch farther in her leg exercises but it would make her work harder and in ballet, harder work made a better dancer. She didn't have music to practice her dancing to. She would use the natural rhythm of the waves to time her *barre* exercises. The sand was firm and good for her feet. Her muscles felt good as they stretched after several days without exercising. Maybe the summer wouldn't be a total waste.

FIVE

~~~

GA-LUMPH ga-lumph ga-losh. The pump made a thumping, whining sound as Zarah worked the handle. The first gush of water was reddish. She dumped it onto the petunias below the porch. They weren't as particular about their bathwater as she was.

When the water ran clear she caught it in a pan and carried it out to the tin washtub she had set in a clearing away from the house. She had a plan.

The outhouse was horrible and she tried not to use it at night but not having hot baths and showers was even worse. Zarah always took long hot soaks in bubbles piled to her chin to ease her aching muscles after ballet workouts or hot massage showers. But to have a hot bath here she had to take the water to the cookshed, heat it on the stove and carry it, buckets and buckets full back to the house or take the tub closer to the cookshed and then she still had to heat the water. This way, she would fill the tub with cold water.

She would let it sit all day and then late in the afternoon, she would have a bath warmed by the sun. She was pleased with her plan. She would get the most out of her labor with the least work possible.

Quanamina shook her head when she saw what Zarah was doing. "You just like somebody else I knowed."

"Who?"

"Just somebody."

Zarah thought her grandmother meant Ila. Ila didn't like to work any more than she had to. But Zarah didn't think many people did. And anyway it was stupid to waste energy. She preferred to use hers on *tour jetes* and *fouettés* and other difficult ballet moves.

Loomis just stared at her with his eyes big. He ran and got his twig broom and carefully raked all around the tub as it sat in the sun while her water warmed.

Zarah could hardly wait until time to take her easy warm bath. But she kept busy sweeping the porches and the house after her workout on the beach.

As the sunlight thinned through the tangle of branches and Spanish moss, Zarah decided it was time. She put on her robe and the red satin mules Londra had given her, collected bath beads, powder and puff, cologne mister, towel, and nightshirt. Loomis and Quanamina were in the cookshed. A screen of bushes hid her from view if they came out. There were no other people on the island. The clearing was her own private bathroom.

What luxury, Zarah thought. A bath *alfresco*. She could loll in the tub and watch the sun go down. She could listen to the birds and wait for the fireflies to flicker in the Spanish moss. She hung the towel and her nightshirt on a bush and arranged her boxes and bottles on a stool she had brought earlier. Then she reached over to test the water and screamed.

A long speckled brown thing was stretched across the surface of the tub. Zarah saw a beady eye. It seemed to be aimed at her. It rippled its awful coils and the water shimmered. She shrieked again and went on shrieking as she backed away from the tub.

"Snake! Snake! Snake!"

Loomis was the first to reach her. "Where? Where?" He jumped around hitting the ground with a stick bigger than he was.

"I'm coming," Quanamina called from the shed.

"There!" Zarah pointed to the center of the tub where the loathsome snake was still rippling the water.

Loomis stopped beating the ground. He squinted at the water. Then he leaned over the tub and picked up the snake. Zarah thought she would faint.

"Don't, Loomis! It will bite you."

"That not a snakey," he said.

"What do you mean that's not a snake. Of course it's a snake. Put it down and kill it before it bites us."

"Not a snakey," Loomis said again.

"Look at it," Zarah began.

"It a toadyfrog," Loomis said.

Quanamina arrived panting. "Where the snake?" She was carrying a hoe.

"It a toadyfrog." Loomis held out his hand with the frog sitting on its haunches in his palm.

Of course it was a frog. She could see it now. "But it looked just like a snake," she said. "It was all stretched out across the water. It seemed long, just like a snake, not like a frog."

Loomis put the frog back in the water. "That how him look swimming."

The frog stretched its legs behind it. It seemed to be floating. It looked like a snake. It looked like a frog. Loomis fished it out again and let it go in the clearing where it hopped away into the bushes.

"Ugh," Zarah said. "It ruined my bathwater."

"Water still good." Quanamina put her hand in it. "Nice and warm."

"I'm not getting in frog water." Zarah tipped the tub over and let the water run across the scratches Loomis's broom had made. "I'll start all over." This time she would have to heat the water and carry it all twice as far.

"Some mules is mighty stubborn," Quanamina said, shaking her head as she made her way back to the cookshed.

SIX

~

HOW YOU fix your hair?" Quanamina called from her room.

"In braids. I put it in braids like you told me," Zarah answered. She had parted her hair in the middle and braided it close to her head all the way from the front to the back and kept going until she ran out of hair. Quanamina stuck her head in the door and nodded with approval when she saw that Zarah's hair was in neat braids. Quanamina went back to her room to finish dressing for church.

Zarah stared at herself in the mirror. The dress Quanamina had made her was horrible. It had puffed sleeves and a full skirt and a sash that tied in the back. The little round collar was edged with white lace. Zarah hadn't worn a dress like that since she was five. She cringed inside the white cotton piqué, starched and ironed by Quanamina into glacial folds.

She couldn't allow herself to be seen like this in public.

It was too humiliating. She was Princess Zarah Brown, future dancer, actor, and talk show personality. She was already a dancer and would be an actor as soon as she could get a part somewhere. Fame would follow. She was not like her mother. She had determination. She scowled at herself. This was definitely not the image she wanted to show the world.

"I look like I'm eight years old," she moaned to the mirror.

"Maybe if my hair didn't look so babyish in these silly braids." She didn't have the nerve to put it in dreadlocks or anything wild. She knew Quanamina would have a fit. But maybe she could decorate the braids a little so she wouldn't be so plain. Her life in New York was theatrical and dramatic. She opened the drawer and pawed through the tangle of Londra's cast-off jewelry.

"You ready?" Quanamina pinned a navy straw hat with pink cabbage roses on the brim to her head with a long hatpin. She picked up a large hatbox.

"Yes, I'm ready." Zarah had made a scarf out of a square of the piqué and tied it neatly under her chin. Her braids were safely hidden, ready for her grand unveiling.

Loomis had on a dark blue suit, a starched white shirt, and a blue and red striped tie. His black shoes were highly polished. He kept leaning over and looking at his reflection in them. Quanamina wore a pink linen dress the same color as the roses on her hat. She had ironed it the day before, heating the iron on the stove in the cookshed. But the dress was already rumpled. It was too tight across Quanamina's stomach and rode upward on her hips and the seat was shiny. But she was a large woman with a strong face. Zarah thought she had presence. She didn't think anyone would ever dare try to conjure Quanamina.

"You look elegant," she said to her grandmother.

Quanamina smiled. "You look sweet."

Zarah decided to take it as a compliment. She followed Loomis and her grandmother down the front porch steps to the river.

"Is the church on the island?" she asked.

"No. It on Barnett."

"Is that an island, too?"

Quanamina nodded.

"How are we going to get there?"

"Junior Simpson come for us in his boat."

"Who's Junior Simpson? Does he run a water taxi?"

"No. He a church member. He look after me. Used to work with Henry some when he a little boy."

Junior was waiting on the bank, one foot propped on an old overturned wooden boat on the narrow beach. He had taken off his white coat and hung it on a tree limb. A small boat with an outboard motor bobbed gently on the river, its nose pointed up on the bank.

"Morning, Miz Mina," Junior greeted them. He wore a straw Panama hat which he lifted before putting his coat back on.

Quanamina introduced them. "This my granddaughter Sarah Jane Brown from New York. She William girl."

Junior shook her hand. "She sure favor."

But Quanamina had said that she looked like Ila, not her father. Maybe she looked like both her parents.

Junior was a tall, good-looking man with a moustache. Zarah thought he must be in his thirties. "We got to hurry. We be late. Brother Zeke don't like latecomers." He helped Quanamina into the boat. Loomis scrambled in. Zarah followed more slowly. She was not happy about this. She had never been in a boat before. It rocked as she stepped in. She grabbed the side and sat down beside Loomis.

"How far do we have to go?"

Junior pushed the boat away from the bank, then jumped in. The boat rocked again as he went to the back and pulled the starter. The motor roared. "Not far. Just over yonder." He pointed to a smudge of low-lying land to the northwest and turned the boat in that direction.

The boat sped across the river, wider here than where she had crossed it on the camel bridge. It didn't look so black in the bright daylight but it was still a river, although Quanamina said it was a tidal river with its unknown currents and inhabitants, alligators, and snakes. Maybe even sharks. Zarah tried not to think about them. Wind tugged at her scarf. She pulled the ends tighter. Waves slapped against the bow. Zarah held onto the side of the boat. She hoped the boat wouldn't break as it smacked against the waves. It was such a little boat.

"It be safe," Loomis whispered.

Zarah looked at him but he wouldn't meet her eyes. He was looking down at the sun shining on his shoe tops.

At last Junior eased the boat up to a wooden dock. Loomis jumped out and tied the bow rope to a post. Zarah climbed out, glad to be on land again. Junior helped Quanamina out of the boat and into a truck waiting on a dirt road that led away from the dock.

Loomis got into the back. Zarah didn't want to but she climbed up and sat beside him on a crate. What an awful vehicle to have to make an entrance from. Zarah's idea of the proper vehicle was a white stretch limo or perhaps a white Porsche 911 with black leather seats. The truck's tailgate was broken and bounced noisily as Junior started it up.

As they drove away from the dock Zarah saw a small store with a gas pump, a telephone booth on the side, and an American flag flying from a pole in front. A sign said BELL'S GROCERY, US POST OFFICE, BARNETT, SC. That must be the store Quanamina mentioned. Zarah wondered if they had batteries. Barnett had electricity. She could see the wires.

They passed small houses similar to Quanamina's. Some were white, some green, some weathered. But no matter what condition the houses were in, they all had freshly painted blue trim around the doors and windows. Zarah decided it must be the style along the coastal islands. The houses had neat garden plots. Most had farm animals, pigs, chickens, cows, horses. One horse had very long ears. It must be a special breed, she decided.

"What kind of horse is that?" she asked Loomis.

He looked at her for so long that she thought he must surely be retarded.

"It a mule," he said solemnly.

The road was unpaved and rutted. Dust billowed behind them as the truck rattled past the houses. Then the road turned to thick creamy sand. The houses gave way to dark woods like those on Domingo. Junior turned into the church-yard and parked under a huge oak tree draped in gray moss.

Loomis jumped from the broken tailgate. Zarah jumped, too. It was quicker than climbing down. Her skirt belled as she landed in a squat in the soft sand. She hoped nobody was watching. She turned around and saw the church. It didn't look like any churches she had ever seen. It was a small white frame building with six wooden columns supporting the overhanging roof in a sort of shallow porch.

Zarah saw four or five cars and two trucks parked in the shade before Junior hurried them into the church. They just had time to sit in the middle of the center of the church before the choir came down the aisles singing, "Praise the Lord, praise him, praise him."

The singers took their places behind the pulpit, massed like the summer sky, Zarah thought, in their light blue robes. Nobody seemed to be looking at her. They probably thought she was Loomis's sister.

The church was filled with people. They must have walked, Zarah decided, because there hadn't been that many cars parked under the trees. The air was stifling with so many people crammed into the small church. The windows were all open but Zarah could smell too many perfumes. Quanamina and other ladies were fanning themselves with woven fans or cardboard paddle fans with pictures of Jesus on one side and DeLong Funeral Parlor advertised on the other.

Zarah never hung out with just African-Americans in New York. She didn't feel any special sense of belonging here. These people were foreign to her, just as Ila had said they would be. In New York she had a scholarship to a private school with an international student body. Some of her friends from ballet school went there, too. Her friends were from Paris, Somalia, Islamabad, Jakarta. Her best friend was Paola from Rome. Londra's friends were a mixture of everything. "It makes life interesting," she always said. Londra had even dated a man from the mountains of Tibet once. "His conversation is loftier than anybody's," she'd joked. "I can't understand a word he says." That was because he only spoke Tibetan.

The minister stood up. "The Lord is in His holy temple. Let us pray." The congregation bowed their heads but Zarah didn't close her eyes. A fly was slowly circling the minister's balding bowed head. If he prayed long enough it might land.

She watched with interest. But he seemed to know the fly was there and said amen just as the fly was about to land.

"Amen," said Quanamina and most of the congregation.

Brother Zeke made some announcements. Then he called for the introduction of visitors. Somebody's brother was visiting from Savannah. Somebody's aunt was here from Edisto. Then Quanamina stood up.

"This my granddaughter, Sarah Jane Brown. William girl from New York City."

"Stand up, Sarah Jane," Brother Zeke said, "and welcome to our flock."

Now it was time for her entrance. Zarah stood up. She wanted to say that her name was Zarah, that she was never going to be Sarah Jane again, it was too plain and ordinary for her but she didn't. She would show them instead. She untied the ends of the scarf and let it fall.

She had attached every one of the sparkling stone earrings of Londra's that she had brought with her. Her braids were covered by a glittering cap of rhinestones, fake rubies, emeralds, and sapphires.

There was an agreeable ooh from some of the younger congregation. Zarah smiled.

But Quanamina wasn't smiling. She was staring at Zarah's head. "Put the scarf back on," she said in a whisper.

When Zarah didn't move, Quanamina reached over and picked it up off the seat where it had fallen. "Put it on," she hissed.

Then she turned to the minister. "Brother Ezekiel, I apologize for my granddaughter. She foreign. She don't know our ways."

She sat down and pulled Zarah down beside her. Loomis peered around from the other side of Quanamina. He looked at her as though he had never seen her before. His eyes were about to jump out of his head. Quanamina pushed him back.

Brother Zeke said another prayer. Then he preached a sermon all about a snake in the heart, the snake of envy, of greed, of dissatisfaction. "Get rid of the snake. All this snake will do is squeeze the life out of the heart that harbors it."

Zarah felt that he was talking to her, that he had improvised the sermon just for her, that he knew she had dissatisfaction in her heart. She didn't want to be on this other-planet island, either of them, Domingo or Barnett. She didn't want to be dressed like an eight-year-old. She wanted drama and excitement. She wanted a career. She was willing to work for it, to sweat blood for it. She wasn't like Ila who wanted it to fall in her lap. Zarah didn't want anything that easy. You had to learn while you worked for success and learning meant making mistakes.

The sermon went on for a long time and then there was more singing. Zarah didn't mind the singing. She sang, "I'm singing for the glory of the Lord," and swayed and clapped with the rest of the congregation. But the seats were hard, it was hot, and she was glad when it was over so they could leave.

Quanamina marched her and Loomis out to the truck without talking to anybody. "Take that jewelry out you hair," she ordered Zarah. "It look common."

"It's not common, it's uncommon," Zarah protested.

"Take it out."

When Zarah didn't move, Quanamina started unhooking the earrings and pulling them out.

"Ouch. You're pulling. I'll do it," Zarah said. With Quanamina and Loomis watching, Zarah removed all the earrings. She tied them up in the scarf and put them inside the crate on the truck. She felt plain and ordinary Sarah Jane again. "Now can we go?" she asked. She didn't want people to see her like this.

"No. We have dinner on the grounds now," Quanamina said.

"Sister Brown! Sister Brown!" Two ladies of the church were marching purposefully toward them.

"Sister Brown, you haven't been to the lodge meetings in a while."

"We missed you at church the last two Sundays."

"I been feeling poorly," Quanamina said.

"This your granddaughter?"

Quanamina introduced her to Sister Beale and Sister Monroe. Sister Monroe wore glasses with gold-wire rims that glinted in the sunlight. The two had straightened gray hair like Quanamina but instead of pulling it into a smooth bun like hers they wore theirs in curls. They were younger than her grandmother, perhaps in their late sixties or early seventies. Their dresses were prim and black. They wore black hats, too, but Sister Monroe's had a rhinestone buckle on the front. Sister Beale's was pierced with a feather, stiff as an arrow.

Their sharp eyes fastened on Zarah. "Who your mama?" Sister Beale asked.

"Ila May," Quanamina said.

"I remember she come here with William after they married. She was a pretty thing."

"She's still pretty," Zarah said.

"Ain't she sweet," Sister Beale said of Zarah. "She the sweetest thing. Your mama married again?"

"No, m'am."

"What she do then?" Sister Beale asked sharply.

"She works as a hostess in a restaurant."

"A hostess?" the two said together.

"Yes, m'am."

It was mostly true. Ila had hostessed at a lot of restaurants. She couldn't stick to anything long. Not even boyfriends. She seemed to lose interest. Except for writing songs. She could do that without thinking, she said. Her songs just happened. It was so easy, all she had to do was write them down. But it didn't earn any money. Ila got her friends to help her make tapes but she never did anything with them. Zarah didn't know how they would live in New York City without her daddy's insurance money and her scholarships.

"Why she didn't come with you?" Sister Beale asked.

"She's working," Zarah said.

Sister Beale pursed her lips.

"It time to eat," Quanamina said.

The hatbox, Zarah discovered, contained a pound cake, still warm from the oven and the South Carolina heat. On the side of the church long tables had been set up, plywood boards on sawhorses. Every family had brought a dish. Zarah saw fried chicken, salads, casseroles, hams, biscuits, rolls, corn bread, pickles, pies, cakes, and iced tea in gallon jugs. There were coolers of ice and some of the children were throwing bits of it until a grown-up chased them away. Quanamina and the other ladies swished the flies.

Brother Zeke gave a long blessing over the food. Zarah thought after all that preaching and praying he might be hungry enough to cut the blessing short but he didn't. She timed him on her snowman watch. A full five minutes.

Quanamina filled a paper plate and helped Loomis fill his. Zarah trailed behind them. Three girls about Zarah's age joined them. Up close they looked younger.

"Miz Mina, did you bring your devil crab?"

"No. I brought pound cake."

"Miz Mina, I just love your devil crab. But your pound cake the best on the island."

"You the best cook anywhere. My mama say so, too."

"This Ernestine, Bina, and Lily," Quanamina said. She and Loomis went over to sit in the shade in chairs set up for the elderly ladies.

"Come sit with us," Ernestine said. Zarah looked back at her grandmother but she was talking with her friends and didn't seem to notice that Zarah wasn't with her. Loomis sat at her feet. He was working on a drumstick.

"OK."

The three girls wore dresses similar to hers except theirs were pastel. Ernestine's was green, Bina's pink, and Lily's was yellow. Zarah was glad they wore different colors because otherwise she wouldn't be able to tell them apart. "Are you sisters?"

They laughed. "No, how could we be? We're the same age," Ernestine said.

"You could be triplets."

They giggled. "We never had any triplets here," Ernestine said.

"We had twins once," Bina said. "The Blivins boys were twins. But they didn't look alike."

"They weren't identical," Lily said in a quiet voice. She seemed shyer than the other two.

"Why you wear your hair like that all covered with earrings?" Ernestine asked.

Zarah didn't want to tell them it was because her dress was so babyish. They wore dresses like that every Sunday.

Besides, Quanamina had made it for her and she had already embarrassed her grandmother enough for one day. "I'm going to be an actor and a dancer. I like to try out different styles."

"You going to be a dancer? And an actor?" Ernestine seemed impressed.

"That's right. This year I'm going to the High School for Performing Arts. That's in New York City. I'm going to have a career."

"Not me," Bina said. "I plan to get married."

"Who to?" Ernestine teased. "Randal?"

Bina giggled. "Maybe."

"I'm going to be a cashier at the Quik-Mart in Beaufort," Ernestine said. "Then I'll get married."

"What about you?" Zarah asked Lily. "Are you going to get married, too?"

"Maybe someday. But I want to be a nurse."

Well, that was something, Zarah thought.

"She all the time saves animals that been hurt," Bina said. "She fixed a 'coon with a broken leg and a lot of birds with broken wings and things."

"Why not a doctor?" Zarah asked her.

"I'll be lucky to be a nurse."

"You can be anything you want to be," Zarah said. "All you have to do is concentrate and ignore everything else."

The three girls blinked. Zarah knew she spoke fiercely. But she believed it. Ila didn't. That was her trouble.

"You'll be a good nurse," she said to Lily. She would be, too, with her soft voice and steady eyes. Zarah thought she would be very comforting to someone who was sick.

"Oh look," Ernestine said. "The Royals are going to sing."

"Who?"

"The Royals. They sing all over South Carolina," Ernestine said.

Big wow, Zarah thought. But she didn't say it.

Junior Simpson was one of the six Royals. Ernestine's mother had brought yellow chenille spreads to sit on. The four girls sat with Ernestine's three little brothers in the shade and listened to the Royals singing gospel songs. The sunlight fell through the sheltering oaks and splashed on the chenille, dappling their skirts spread around them like flowers and their bare brown legs. Their voices fluttered around her, soft as butterflies.

After the Royals, there was more singing by other groups, some from other churches, more eating. By the time Junior loaded them into the boat for the trip back to Domingo, the sun was sinking into the marsh. Zarah felt tired from the salt breeze, the sun, and too much food. Her hated dress now hung in limp folds. She scratched at a mosquito bite. She still had the chenille pattern imprinted on her legs. She was too tired to be as scared as she had been on the earlier trip.

"The tide coming in," Junior said. "We can ride it back."

The wind had dropped and the waves didn't seem to slap the boat quite as hard this time. Zarah was glad for the smoother ride.

As Junior helped Quanamina out of the boat on Domingo, Loomis handed Zarah the scarf with the earrings tied up in it. "It pretty," Loomis whispered.

This was the second time he had spoken to her today.

"Thanks, Loomis." Maybe he wasn't retarded, she thought.

SEVEN

~~~~~

ZARAH waited for Quanamina to lecture her but all her grand-mother said was, "Why you shame me, child?" She was snapping beans on the back porch.

"Shame you? What was shameful about decorating my hair so I didn't look babyish?"

"You make yourself stand out." *Snap snap.* "Make a spectacle of yourself in church." *Snap snapsnapsnap snap.*

Zarah didn't see anything shameful about that. "I can't be plain," she said. "I have to be Zarah. I have to stand out. I don't want to be like everybody else."

Quanamina didn't reply, just went on snapping those beans like castanets. Loomis was scratching at the dirt with his twig broom. *Snap snap. Scratch Scratch.* Even the frizzle chicken was making pecking sounds with its beak. Zarah thought all the clicking, snapping, scratching sounds would make her scream. She went down the steps to escape to the beach.

"What you go to the beach every day?" Quanamina asked. Quanamina never questioned Zarah about her life in New York. She only asked about things on the island.

"I go to the beach to practice my dance exercises," Zarah said. "I don't want to get behind my class. And I walk on the beach. The sand is very good for a dancer's feet. It makes them stronger and massages them."

Zarah waited for her to say something, to comment on Zarah's dedication to her art but Quanamina went on snapping beans. Finally she said, "Tip out that dishpan on the flowers."

The pan stood near the pump on a crude table. Zarah let the water cascade onto the pink and lavender petunias growing beside the back steps. The weight flattened some of them. Blue morning glories escaped up the porch railings. Sky eyes, Loomis called them. Zarah hung the dishpan on a nail beside the kitchen door and went down the back steps.

She was sorry that Quanamina felt shamed. But she couldn't be plain. She just couldn't. She had to be Zarah. Maybe not Princess Zarah. Not all the time. But she couldn't be Sarah Jane.

Zarah found her snake stick and followed the beach path. She knew to avoid the lacy tendrils of gray Spanish moss now. Chiggers lived in them. Zarah had never heard of chiggers before but now she knew all about them. They burrowed in the skin and itched like fire. Quanamina had her dip her finger in water, then in salt and rub it on the red lumps where the chiggers had gone in. To her amazement, it worked and the terrible itching stopped every time.

She jogged along the beach to the palm roots she used for a *barre* beside the little creek. She liked walking on the beach. She felt safer there than on the wooded paths. She didn't think snakes would crawl on the hot white sand or in the edge of the salt water. And if they did, she could see them easily. Quanamina said that rattlesnakes didn't always rattle and copperheads didn't always look like leaves. Sometimes they changed color, she said. But Zarah didn't think they could turn as pale as the sand.

Zarah started her *pliés*, *demi* and then *grand* all the way down to a squat. Then she moved on to *tendues*.

"What are you doing?" Zarah thought she heard a voice say. She'd been without normal conversation so long that she was now imagining voices. She shook her head and pointed her foot.

"Are you doing ballet?" the voice asked.

Zarah looked around. On the other side of the little creek was a girl. Zarah was startled. The girl was real, not something in her imagination. She was tall but looked about Zarah's age. She wore cutoffs and a tank top just as Zarah did. She had long dark brown hair and brown eyes.

"Yes. I'm doing my daily workout," Zarah replied without stopping her *tendues*.

"Can I watch?"

Zarah shrugged. "If you like." She wouldn't interrupt her workout, not even for this. Discipline was important in ballet, in acting, in any of the arts, Zarah believed. It was what Ila, for all her talent, lacked. She moved on to the *rond de jambe*.

The girl sat on the trunk of an uprooted palm and watched quietly until Zarah had finished her workout.

Zarah was sweating even in the cool sea breeze. She backed down the beach, then ran toward the creek. When she reached it, she leaped over the clear water in a *grand jeté*.

"Brava!" The girl clapped. Zarah sat down beside her on the palm. "You're good," the girl said.

"I work for it," Zarah told her.

"Do you live here?"

"No. I live in New York City. I'm visiting my grandmother."

"Me, too. My name is Benicia O'Neil." She was from California, near San Francisco. "We go to the ballet there sometimes," she added.

"I'm Princess Zarah."

Benicia stared at her. "Are you really a princess?"

Zarah tossed her head. "It's my soul name. My legal name is Sarah Jane Brown. You can call me Zarah. In New York, everybody does."

Benicia's grandparents were the Saylors of Saylor's Island. "I live on a ranch in California. We raise and train palominos." She paused. "It's real different here."

"I know what you mean."

"It's like being on Mars or in Tahiti or somewhere."

"That's how I feel, too," Zarah said.

"I've got this awful fourth cousin or something like that," Benicia said. "I mean, whoever counts such things. All she wants to do is dress up and go shopping or to lunch somewhere. She isn't real. Everybody calls her by two names, Mary Saylor. They run it together, Marysaylor. She talks about clothes and boys all the time. She's going to be a debutante. It's so bor-ing."

Zarah thought about Bina and Ernestine. They would probably be like that if they were white and rich. Lily was different. "Yeah. Feminism is probably a bad word here."

"It really is. I said something about ERA and my grandfather said, 'Those outsiders are always stirring up trouble.' "

Zarah laughed.

"Why were you practicing on the beach? Don't you need music for ballet?"

"Yeah. But I don't have any batteries for my Walkman. I can do my workouts to the rhythm of the waves. But I'm starving for my music. I brought most of my tapes but now I can't play them."

"Why not?"

"Nowhere to plug in and I didn't bring any spare batteries."

Benicia jumped up. "We can play them at my grandmother's house."

"OK. I'll get them. Wait here." Zarah leaped over the stream again and ran up the beach before Benicia could follow. She didn't want to have to explain anything to Quanamina. She had a feeling that Quanamina would say no.

No one was in the house when Zarah got there. She took time to change into clean shorts and a fresh red T-shirt, grabbed the bag of tapes, and ran back to the beach. She was so glad to have music again and somebody to talk to from her world that she hardly bothered about snakes.

Benicia was waiting at the end of the path. "Domingo and Saylor used to be one island," Benicia said as they crossed the little stream that divided the islands. "But it was a long time ago. It was discovered by a Spanish explorer in the 1520s. He named it Domingo because it was a Sunday and that means Sunday in Spanish."

"I know that. I've had Spanish." And Ila had made up a song, "Domingo Is the Sunday of My Dreams."

"When the English came, the Saylor family got the island from the king. They changed the name to Saylor. A storm opened the creek to the ocean sometime after that and turned it into two islands. I guess people went back to the old name for Domingo. Domingo was a lot bigger then."

"You seem to know a lot about this place."

"My grandmother tells me all this stuff. She's writing it all down and hopes to get it published someday. She talks about it all the time. There isn't much else to do here."

"Yeah, tell me about it."

"My grandmother says I need to know my heritage. It's interesting but it doesn't have anything to do with me."

Zarah thought about her heritage and realized that her ancestors had been slaves of Benicia's ancestors. She stared at Benicia. She thought she should feel something, antagonism, hate, or at least discomfort. But she didn't. She was just glad to have somebody from the real world to talk to, to listen to tapes with. She was accustomed to Londra's and her mother's friends in the arts, musicians, aspiring actors, poets, dancers. She didn't even know how to talk to girls like Ernestine and Bina. "I know. I don't feel connected to this place either. Sometimes I can hardly understand the way they talk, especially the old people."

"That's Gullah," Benicia said. "I can't understand it either but my grandparents can. It's really sort of another language. The words are mostly English but they are put together differently, more like African and a little Arabic and Portuguese because they were the slave traders." Then she looked embarrassed. "I'm sorry. I shouldn't have said that."

"Hey, that's nothing to do with me," Zarah said. "Nobody can change history. Besides, I was never a slave."

"Well," Benicia said slowly, "I guess my ancestors were slave owners, the Saylors and others. But I never knew it until this summer when I came here. But you're right. It all happened a long time ago. We only have to worry about now."

"And that's enough," Zarah said. Benicia laughed.

"One thing I can't figure out," Zarah said. "Some of the houses down here haven't been painted since the Civil War but the doorways and windowsills have been freshly painted bright blue. Does your grandmother know why?"

"Sure. That's to keep evil spirits out. You know, witches and things."

At Zarah's incredulous look she explained, "The blue represents water. Witches can't cross water. They'll drown or something. A lot of people believe that around here."

But not the Saylors. It fit with the frizzle chicken and the conjure bags, the hu hu and tying knots in a bedsheet. The Saylors were above all that. They probably were Episcopalian, Zarah thought. No amens and clapping in church for them.

The house at Saylor's Landing was built in the seventeen hundreds, Benicia told her. "Before the revolution. After, Lafayette visited the house. It's famous. People come all the time to take pictures and put it in books. Architecture classes come to study it."

"General Lafayette? The one that came to help George Washington?"

"That's the one."

She followed Benicia up the double curving stairs to the small porch. She smiled to herself when she saw the seashells carved over the door, symbols of water, plantation style.

Zarah was expecting something really grand. She was surprised at how actually small the house was. She expected all plantations to look like Tara in *Gone with the Wind* even though she knew it wasn't even a real house. She didn't know anything about architecture but she could see that the Saylors' house was well designed. Inside it seemed bigger, probably because of the high ceilings. The rooms were airy and spacious. There were four levels, cellar, two floors, and an attic with dormer windows.

She noticed the smell first, lemon and wax and something sweet like gardenia or jasmine. And everything seemed to gleam as though little bits of light had been stuck to the glass, the silver, brass, the pine floors, mahogany table tops, and even the satin damask pillows on sofas and chairs. There were vases of fresh flowers all around, big bunches of mixed colors.

No wonder they fought a war to keep it, Zarah thought. But what about the ones who didn't live in the big house. She'd read about the Civil War. There were more dirt farmers whose lives weren't much better than slaves. They also fought to keep slavery, even though they didn't have any slaves. There was just no accounting for people. She followed Benicia up the stairs with the dark mahogany railing curving like a snake. She felt like she was walking into history.

Benicia's room looked like a picture in a magazine, too, canopied four-poster bed, mahogany furniture, a marble fireplace. The room was done in salmon and soft green with splashes of paprika to punch up the color scheme as Londra's decorator friends would say. They suited Benicia better than the pastels downstairs.

"What a room," she said in her Bette Davis voice. "It's gorgeous."

"I feel like I'm living in a museum," Benicia said, shrugging.

"Yeah. I know what you mean. I feel like that at my

grandmother's only for different reasons. I didn't know people lived in this country without electricity and plumbing."

Benicia opened a cabinet. Inside was a tape player. "Let's listen to your tapes."

Zarah gave her the one Ila called "Birdsongs." Benicia read the title. She didn't say anything as she slid the tape in place and pressed the play button. She was in for a surprise. The songs were all about birds, all right, but not the birds Benicia was expecting. The first one was "Jive Turkey Blues." "When your day goes aground, and there's trouble all around, you got the jive turkey blues."

Zarah laughed at the expression on Benicia's face when she realized what the song was about.

After awhile Benicia said, "I didn't expect them to be so funny. Is your mother famous?"

"No. Why would you think that?"

"Well, she writes great songs and they're recorded."

"Taped. These aren't professional demos." Zarah danced around a green moiré chair, all ripply like water.

Benicia followed her. "What's the difference?"

"She's not a professional. Professional means finding out what works. Ila does what she likes, whatever pleases her."

"That sounds professional to me."

"It's what you do with them. You have to make a demo, get an agent, get DJ's to play them, things like that. It's not as easy as writing words and notes on paper."

"She should be professional then. Her songs are good. I like 'The Sparrow That Ate New York' best."

"Play this one." Zarah gave Benicia the tape Ila called "Manhattan Hippos." It was real jazzy. The two girls danced to the music, snapping their fingers to the beat. They danced around the chairs, around the canopied bed, in front of the windows with their pale green curtains belling in the breeze like branches of trees.

"Benicia, what is going on in here? That awful racket . . ." The woman's voice trailed off as she caught sight of Zarah dancing by the window. Zarah stopped.

"We're just listening to Zarah's tapes, Grandmother," Benicia said. "This is Zarah Brown. Zarah, this is my grandmother, Mrs. Saylor."

Zarah started to offer her hand but she realized that Mrs. Saylor wouldn't take it. She stood very still and played Grace Kelly in her princess roles. "How do you do, Mrs. Saylor."

Mrs. Saylor was a small woman with small bones. Ila would write a song about her. The small gray wren with bones of steel, hair arranged in a silver helmet. Her eyes were pale blue-gray. She wore a blue-flowered skirt and blouse and low-heeled white sandals. Her legs were thin and bone white, streaked with blue veins like marble.

"Zarah is visiting her grandmother on Domingo," Benicia said.

"Yes, I know. Quanamina told me she was here. You will have to excuse us," she said to Zarah. "Benicia, dear, Grace is expecting us for lunch. Please change into something suitable. I'll be waiting downstairs."

She didn't look at Zarah. But their eyes met in the mirror. Her eyes were more gray than blue, Zarah realized, as though the blue had faded, leaving only the frowning gray. They looked through Zarah, as though she wasn't there. Zarah made her eyes as haughty as she could, Glenda Jackson as Elizabeth I. Mrs. Saylor looked away first.

"I'm sorry," Benicia began when Mrs. Saylor had gone downstairs.

"It's OK. Not your fault."

"I didn't know we had to go to Aunt Grace's."

"It's all right. Don't worry about me. My grandmother will be wondering where I am."

"Listen, I'm having a party a week from Saturday. Do you think you can come?"

"Well, I don't know," Zarah began but Benicia interrupted her. "Oh, please come. I won't know anybody but that drip Mary Saylor. The others will probably be just like her. If you come it won't be so bad."

"OK. I'll have to consult my calendar to be sure but I think that date is free."

Benicia giggled. "Where else could you go around here?"

"The Birdsong Ballet?" Zarah suggested.

"Yeah, right."

"What kind of party is it?"

"A dinner party. But afterward we can dance."

Zarah rolled her eyes. "Your grandmother won't like that."

"Oh, she'll let us. That's what is done at parties. She'll put up with the racket if it's what's done."

Zarah thought it would be an interesting evening. She bet Mrs. Saylor would be furious if she showed up at the party. But Benicia had invited her. She gathered her tapes.

"I'll get you some batteries," Benicia said. "It will only take a minute. Then you won't have to practice to the sound of waves."

"I like it," Zarah said. But she accepted the batteries. It would be good to have music again.

EIGHT

~~~~~~

QUANAMINA and Loomis came back late in the afternoon carrying cane poles and a bucket of fish.

"Catch me some water," Quanamina told Loomis. To Zarah she said, "We had good luck. Fish bite good."

"What kind of fish are they?" Zarah could see silvery flashes in the bucket of muddy water.

"Mullet."

Zarah had never heard of a fish called mullet. "Are they like mahimahi or Dover sole?"

Quanamina looked at her as if she had never heard of those fish. "They good," she said.

She and Loomis cleaned the fish out behind the chicken pen, then threw the entrails over the wire. The chickens ran all over each other trying to get the pink and yellow globules.

Disgusting. Zarah watched from the porch. She thought chickens were stupid creatures. Fish insides were pretty awful, too. She didn't plan to eat any of the mullet.

The frizzle chicken hurried over to the pen to see what the excitement was. It ran around outside trying to get in, reminding Zarah of Ila's song, "Funky Chicken Fugue." Ila must have been thinking about frizzle chickens when she wrote it.

The frizzle chicken tried to tear at the wire of the pen with its beak. "Stupid thing. You're free and you want to get in the pen." The other chickens were just as stupid. They didn't seem to know they were in a pen.

Zarah didn't tell Quanamina about meeting Benicia. She didn't mean not to tell her. It just never came up. She had a feeling that Quanamina wouldn't want her to go over to the Saylors'. She had never mentioned them to Zarah, but she talked to Mrs. Saylor sometimes. Zarah wondered what her grandmother said about her.

Quanamina cooked the fish in a black iron frying pan on the wood stove in the shed. She called it smutter fish. It didn't sound appetizing but it smelled so good that Zarah forgot she wasn't going to eat any. The fish was smothered in a thick gravy flavored with onions. There were fried cakes that Loomis called hush puppies and fresh tomatoes and cucumbers in vinegar. Quanamina had made blackberry cush for dessert. It was sort of like a cobbler, Zarah discovered, and just as good.

"The girls over on Barnett were right," she said as she scraped the last bit of cush into her spoon. "You are the best cook anywhere."

"Food always taste good when you hungry." Quanamina said. But she smiled as she said it.

Loomis helped Zarah wash the dishes. It was as difficult as getting a bath. Zarah washed them in a pan of dishwater that had to be pumped at the house, carried to the cookshed and heated to boiling, then brought to the kitchen again where soap was added. The washed dishes were rinsed by dunking them into another pan of cool pump water. Then Loomis dried them and put them away. Zarah was hot and sticky by the time she finished, her T-shirt glued to her back. Just getting a meal was a lot of work without running water and electricity.

They sat on the screened front porch watching night fall. Zarah had never just sat and watched dark replace light until she came to Domingo. She had always been busy with schoolwork, reading, talking on the phone to her friends, trying new hairstyles, watching TV, or listening to tapes or the radio. Anyway, the lights in New York came on before dusk so you could hardly tell when it was getting dark there.

She had always thought that nightfall would be a quiet time in the country away from rush hour traffic and other city noises. The word nightfall even sounded soft and quiet. But in its way nightfall on Domingo was just as noisy as New York. Birds screamed as they looked for a safe comfortable tree for the night. And the insects almost drowned out the birds. But gradually the island settled down until only the songs of the frogs and crickets were left.

Fireflies blinked on and off in the woods surrounding the house, turning all the trees along the edge of the clearing into Christmas trees with their own twinkle lights. It seemed to be a good time to ask Quanamina some questions. Zarah started with a simple one.

"Quanamina, why does Domingo have a different name from Saylor?"

Quanamina didn't answer right away. The rocker creaked back and forth, back and forth. Then Quanamina said, "My great-grandmother Zalinda was brought over from Africa, princess there, slave here. She have a girl by Arab trader. That girl Shakirah. Shakirah very beautiful. Her girl name Shalenah. She marry James Washington. James buy this land from the government after the war."

"Which war was that?" asked Zarah, thinking of World War II.

"War that free the slaves."

With a shock Zarah realized that Quanamina was talking about events that happened more than a hundred years before. The war was the Civil War. It had ended in 1865. This was 1982, a hundred and seventeen years later.

"Domingo part of Saylor Island then. It all one plantation then. James buy forty acres from creek to sea. It old name Domingo. That mean Sunday. James change it back cause he say everyday like Sunday when man free working for himself. And it been Domingo ever since."

Zarah felt herself under a spell as she listened to her grandmother talk about her ancestors. Ila never talked about the past any further back than her childhood and not much of that. And only when it suited her purpose. Zarah was sure she made some of her stories up. But Quanamina was telling true stories about people she was descended from.

"If Zalinda was a princess, does that mean I'm a princess, too?"

"I don't know, child. We don't have princess here. If you go to Africa, maybe you be princess there."

Zarah didn't think she wanted to go to Africa. Not now. She only wanted to go to New York and become a dancer and actor. She wanted to be a princess of the stage in America. She had always been a princess in her own mind. That was what was important, what she thought she was.

A loud bellow sounded in the darkness that surrounded them now. "What was that?"

"Alligator."

"On the island?" Zarah's voice rose to a squeak.

"In the black swamp. They won't hurt you, you stay away from 'em."

"They don't have to worry about me. I'll stay away from them and the black swamp and the white swamp, too."

Quanamina got up and lit the kerosene lamp. The light shone on her arms, which were as smooth as the polished mahogany in the Saylors' house and cast their shadows larger than life on the wall of the house.

Zarah thought about Princess Zalinda. "That would make Loomis a prince, wouldn't it?"

"Reckon so. He my grandson."

Loomis looked up at the mention of his name. He was playing with strings, putting them into intricate patterns. "Look," he said. The strings were woven on his fingers in a cat's cradle.

"Where did you learn to do that?"

"Mina. She usta make basket till her hand get stiff with misery."

Zarah watched his nimble fingers weaving the lacy patterns. "I never could do that," she said.

"I show you," Loomis said almost in a whisper. "It easy."

He placed the strings on Zarah's fingers. His touch was as light as the string.

While the frogs croaked and the crickets sang, Loomis taught Zarah how to weave a spiderweb of string around her fingers in ancient African patterns while moths batted softly against the screens, drawn there by the circle of light.

NINE

~~~~~

WHAT DO you think of this shade?" Benicia asked Zarah. She held up a tube of bright magenta. They were trying out makeup at the dressing table in Benicia's room.

"Let me see." Zarah looked at the color critically.

"No, I think you need something pinker."

"It will look great on you." Benicia's cousin Mary Saylor Harkness had given her a bag of old cosmetics she didn't use anymore. "She's only fifteen and already has more makeup than a clown."

Benicia didn't know much about makeup but Zarah did. Londra had taught her. "My best friend at home is a boy." Benicia giggled. "He would think I was crazy if he could see me now."

Her eyelids were rainbows of shades of purple. Zarah had showed her how to stroke the different shades on from light to dark to light. Zarah's own lids were orange. She'd wanted to sprinkle gold dust on them but was afraid it would get in her eyes.

"You try it." Benicia held the lipstick out to Zarah.

"It will clash with my eyelids and lose. It should be more purple to stand up to the orange."

"Are you going to wear makeup to my party?"

"Sure. Not a lot though. Not this much. I wear it all the time in New York."

"I will, too. My grandmother will be scandalized. She says that a lot. Scandalized."

They giggled at the thought of Benicia's scandalized grandmother.

"She scandalizes easily," Zarah said. "My grandmother does, too."

"Grandmothers are weird. I wonder if they were always like that or if it only happens when they become grand-mothers?"

"Beats me," Zarah said.

Mrs. Saylor was at a meeting in Charleston. Zarah hadn't been back to the Saylors' since the day she met Benicia but they met every day on the beach after Zarah finished her workout. The beach was neutral ground. They could do and say what they wanted to away from the disapproving eyes of their grandmothers. They swam in the ocean but neither would go far out. There were things to watch out for on land and sea—snakes, spiders, alligators, chiggers in the Spanish moss, crabs, and sharks. And then Benicia told her about jellyfish and men-of-war. And ghosts.

"My grandmother says there is a ghost that walks on this beach in broad daylight."

"Ghosts don't come out in daylight. Everybody knows that."

"This one does. She walks the beach because her fiancé was coming to their wedding by boat and it capsized and he drowned. She grieved herself to death. It was over a hundred years ago."

"Yeah. Women did that a lot in those days. There weren't enough men to go around so they died of grief. It was more socially acceptable than poison or a bullet. And it gave them status." Zarah put on her southern belle accent. "I declare, Josephine-Marie is jus' pinin' away for Whitney Benedict." She put her wrist to her forehead.

Benicia giggled. "Hey, you really are an actress."

"Actor. Actress sounds, well too actressy. I told you. I practice that, too. So what happened? The ghost pined away?"

"And whenever something bad is going to happen like a storm or an accident, somebody always sees the ghost on the beach."

"This beach?"

"This one," Benicia said.

"Who sees this ghost?"

"My grandmother says she saw her on the afternoon before the hurricane of 1944 that killed a lot of people on the islands."

"Did she tell anybody before the hurricane hit?"

"Well, no. I don't think so. I don't know. But she told them after. She remembered seeing a woman in a long gray dress walking on the beach and wringing her hands as though in sorrow. She saw her from the attic window of the house."

"Do you believe it?"

"I believe my grandmother saw something she thinks was a ghost. It could have been something that blew up in the wind, I guess. Spanish moss, maybe."

"Probably." Zarah thought about Quanamina's frizzle chicken and the conjure bags. "My grandmother believes in ghosts, too. My little cousin, Loomis, is scared silly of them. My grandmother won't let me mention anything that might scare Loomis."

"Everybody believes in spirits down here. Mary Saylor tells me ghost stories all the time."

"Do you know what a hu hu is?"

"Sure. It's an owl. To hear one means bad luck or that someone is going to die."

No wonder Loomis was such a shy, scared little boy, Zarah thought. He never knew when a snake or an alligator or a ghost was going to get him.

~~~~~~~~~

ZARAH planned to wear her purple Charmeuse dress to the party. No way was she going to wear that white baby dress again. After that Sunday at church Quanamina had washed and ironed it and hung it in Zarah's room. Every time she opened the chifforobe the white dress was hanging there like a starched ghost. Zarah had pushed it to the back but she still knew it was there. She could see the sleeves puffed with self-importance behind the riotous colors of the clothes Londra had given her.

She waited until Saturday afternoon to tell Quanamina about the party. Her grandmother didn't object. "Wear the white dress," was all she said.

"I'm not going to wear that dress to a party. It's all wrong for a party." Zarah had washed her hair and was combing it dry in the sun on the back steps.

"It a nice dress."

"Nobody in the real world wears dresses like that. Everybody will laugh at me."

"No they won't. You be in the kitchen with me most of the time."

Zarah stopped combing and stared at her grandmother. "What do you mean I'll be in the kitchen with you?"

"I mean that where you be. Miz Saylor want you to serve and help in the kitchen."

"But I'm a guest. Benicia invited me. I'm not a slave."

"She pay you."

"What difference does that make? I am an invited guest. Her granddaughter invited me. I'm not a servant."

"It Miz Saylor house. She say you serve. That what you do." Quanamina tied a white apron over her black cotton maid's dress. "I need you help. I be too old do it alone. Loomis help some but not enough."

The anger in Zarah's heart was bitter and strong enough to spawn a million snakes. How could Quanamina do this to her? And Benicia. She would never speak to Benicia again. How could she? And that vile old grandmother of hers. Zarah jerked her thoughts away from Mrs. Saylor. She stomped to her room and slammed the door as hard as she could. The whole house shook.

Quanamina went early to the Saylors' to start the cooking. Zarah sulked in her room but she put on the hated white dress and did her hair in a single French braid.

"Mina say you wear this." Loomis handed her a black apron. Zarah put it on but she had her own plans.

Loomis saw her putting things into her Bloomingdale bag. His eyes widened as she threw in handfuls of jewelry.

"Don't you say a word about this," she told him. "If you do the hu hu will get you."

His eyes got bigger. He looked scared but he shook his head. He was silent as they walked over to the Saylors' but he stayed close to her. Zarah left the Bloomingdale bag behind a camellia bush near the back door of the Saylors' house. The kitchen was in the cellar. That meant Zarah had to carry everything up a flight of stairs to the dining room. But first she had to put a red-checked apron over the black one which Quanamina called a serving apron and help her grandmother with the cooking. Zarah chopped celery and parsley and onions which made her eyes water. It felt good to cry even though her eyes burned uncomfortably. "I'm not crying," she said to Loomis as he peeled the shells off hard-boiled eggs. "It's the onions."

Mrs. Saylor came down to check on the food.

"It's so nice you can help your grandmother, Sarah Jane."

Zarah didn't answer, just went on chopping onions. Mrs. Saylor turned back to Quanamina. "Has that lawyer been bothering you again?"

"Not since last time."

"Well, you just tell him to see us if he bothers you. We can't let developers destroy our islands the way they did the others."

What lawyer? What developers? Zarah waited for more but Quanamina was measuring flour and didn't answer. Mrs. Saylor went upstairs with a swish of her blue skirt.

Zarah washed pots and pans while Quanamina cooked. Chicken casserole, baked ham with pineapple, rice, butter beans, congealed salad, chocolate cake, and homemade ice cream. Mr. Saylor and a black man Zarah didn't know made the ice cream. Loomis was allowed to lick the dasher. They asked Zarah, too, but she refused. She would never eat a bite at this house unless she was sitting with a snowy damask napkin in her lap at the long shiny table under the blazing crystal chandelier in the dining room.

She didn't see Benicia until she served the food. The dinner was buffet style. The guests filled their plates at the long sideboard, then sat at the dining table and several smaller tables set up in the living room. There were white candles and fresh flowers on the tables just like she'd seen in magazines. But to Zarah's eyes it was all ugly. The candles shed no light upon her and the flowers were racist blooms.

She took a platter of sliced ham surrounded with pineapple slices and pickled peaches to the sideboard. For two cents she would tilt it and let all the ham slide onto the carpet. But she caught herself. Her plan was much better. She carried all the food except the dessert up to the dining room and arranged it on the long buffet table. The guests were out on the terrace. It didn't sound like much of a party. Zarah couldn't hear any talking or laughing. She took the empty tray back downstairs and helped Quanamina remove two chocolate cakes from the oven.

Mrs. Saylor came to the kitchen twice to ask for more biscuits. "And Sarah Jane, pass the biscuits around at the tables this time."

Zarah gave her the Queen Elizabeth I look and took the silver bread tray that Quanamina had filled with hot biscuits wrapped in a linen napkin. She went up the stairs with her back as stiff as if she had a broom handle for a spine. She went first to the dining room. Benicia, in a pale blue dress, was sitting at the head of the table. A red-headed boy sat on one side, a pale blond on the other. They looked bored. Benicia looked embarrassed, keeping her eyes on her plate. Zarah marched straight up to Benicia. Now she had to look up and see Zarah.

"Mo' biscuits, miss," she said in a Butterfly McQueen voice.

Benicia looked at her, blushed, and looked away. Zarah made the round of the table. The boys were talking about sports, the girls about clothes. They stopped talking when Zarah offered the biscuits. They were all about her age. Zarah ignored them and concentrated on playing the part of a maid on a stage, a French maid from Martinique.

After dessert Zarah only had to finish washing the pots and pans. Mrs. Saylor didn't want to trust her fine crystal and china and silver to Zarah's inexpert hands and Quanamina had arthritis. Mrs. Saylor would do those herself. The party had waned after the food was gone. Zarah could hear its silence up the stairs. Nobody was talking. Slow fifties music oozed out of the stereo in the living room.

"Why don't you all go out on the terrace and dance?" Mrs. Saylor suggested as Zarah cleared the tables. Benicia winced. There were embarrassed giggles but the party straggled through the French doors. Zarah went back down to the kitchen with the last load of plates. She finished scraping them into a bag to take back to Quanamina's chickens. Then she slipped away while Loomis was sweeping the kitchen floor. It would be dark in a few minutes.

She found her Bloomingdale's bag and changed behind the bush into the costume she'd concocted out of Londra's old animal print scarves. Nobody could see her from the house and behind her were dark woods. She unbraided her hair, fluffed and spritzed it with water she'd brought in a spray bottle. She wanted it to look wild. She anchored a pendant so that it hung across her forehead. Gold bracelets from wrists to elbows and on her ankles. Gold eye shadow, gold lipstick, black mascara, and she was ready. She slid in a tape and turned up the sound on her Walkman. The music of "Zulu Moon" vibrated through the night with savage drums, drowning out the crickets and frogs.

Her cue was a Tarzanlike yell. Zarah leaped out of the bushes. The bored faces ranged around the terrace were startled, then interested. Zarah spun into her own version of a dance. She could dance any style, jazz, tap, modern, even belly dancing besides ballet. She hadn't practiced this dance. She knew her emotions would make her creative. This was a dance from her heart, both sinuous and frenzied at the same time. She had held her anger in until this moment. Now she channeled it into the dance, spinning, vaulting, a gazelle, a lion, a panther, a tiger, both hunter and hunted. Her bare feet clung to the bricks of the terrace as though she had prehensile toes. The brief thought that her ancestors had made those bricks, that Zalinda had swept them fueled her dance.

The party was electrified. Zarah's intensity charged into the crowd. She leaped higher, whirled, challenged, her face set in a haughty stare. The guests began clapping, swaying, moving with her beat. Benicia smiled, snapping her fingers.

The music ended with a discordant crash. Zarah stopped dead and then walked away, her back to them.

"Wow!" someone said.

"Benicia! What is going on?" Mr. and Mrs. Saylor and two other parents appeared at the door. Quanamina was behind them. Zarah saw Loomis duck behind a bush.

"Zarah was entertaining us," Benicia said. She flashed Zarah a look of thanks as the tape clicked to the other side and the music began again. The party came to life and everyone started dancing to "Nairobi Nights."

One of the boys asked Zarah to dance but she heard

Quanamina say, "Zarah," her face a mask carved out of some dark African wood, darker than mahogany, a mask of disapproval.

"I have to go," she said. She stopped the tape and ejected it. If she took the tape away, the party would die again. She alone had the power to save it. She paused, deciding. Benicia had given her several packs of batteries so she wouldn't run out, she said. But Zarah knew it was so she wouldn't have to ask for them. "Here," she held the tape out to Benicia.

"Put it on your grandmother's stereo," Zarah told her.

Benicia moved to do it and atonal notes flowed into the beat. "Now that's music," she heard someone say as she left the party.

"And dancing. She was great."

"I've never seen anybody dance like that," somebody else said.

Zarah changed back into the dress and apron, slid her feet into her flats, and went back to the kitchen. Quanamina and Loomis were ready to go. Quanamina was carrying a box. Loomis had the bag for the chickens. Quanamina didn't say a word as they walked back through the woods. Loomis led the way with the flashlight Mr. Saylor had loaned them. In the darkness behind them Zarah heard an alligator roar. But he wasn't nearly as fearsome as Quanamina.

At the house Quanamina pulled herself up the steps by the railing. She seemed heavier tonight. Her feet were like great stones that she could hardly lift. She stopped at the top of the steps and stood there breathing hard as though the darkness had been too thick and she had exhausted herself just walking through it.

After a minute she told Loomis to light her way into the

house. The flashlight made strange, grotesque shadows on the walls and for a minute Zarah could almost believe in spirits and conjure. Then Quanamina lit the lamp and the darkness went away. With it went her breathlessness but she still seemed tired.

"I got to sit down. I be too old," she said. "Go with Loomis to put the food up."

Zarah followed Loomis and the flashlight to the well house. There, sunk in the ground, was a Styrofoam cooler with ice in it. When Quanamina had mentioned the icebox, Zarah had thought she meant the old-fashioned kind she'd seen in museums, not a picnic cooler buried in the ground. But she supposed it made sense. The ice wouldn't melt as fast with the ground as a natural insulator.

"Where does she get ice?" she asked Loomis.

"Junior bring it. With the milk."

"When does he come?"

"Every other day. Morning mostly."

Before she was awake, Zarah guessed. She put the food in the box with a carton of milk and several small plastic containers. She put the lid on tightly.

"Come on. Let's go back."

Near the house they heard a fluttering noise. Loomis jumped and grabbed Zarah's skirt.

"That a hu hu?"

She touched his shoulder. "It was only the frizzle chicken," she told him. "We woke him up."

Loomis giggled. She kept her hand on his shoulder all the way to the house. His shoulders were narrow, the bones thin as kite sticks. He was afraid of so many things—spirits, conjure, hu hus, snakes. But he'd come to her rescue that day when the frog was in her bath.

Quanamina was still in the chair. She stayed there, even after Loomis went to bed.

Zarah waited for Quanamina to let her have it. She braced herself.

Finally Quanamina said, "I never thought I'd see you when you daddy die. Then you come here and shame me. Now you shame me again, child."

"How?" The words burst out. "What did I do to shame you?"

"You suppose to serve, not dance."

"I didn't shame you. I was invited to that party. I'm not the Saylors' slave."

"No, you not. You got paid."

"I'm not a servant either."

"That what you got paid for."

"I did the work."

"You not supposed to dance. That for guest."

"I entertained. There's a difference. That's why I danced. I had to show them I'm a dancer, not a servant. And I'm a good one. I'm not like Ila. I don't just dream. I do something about my dreams. I practice. I work hard. This fall I'm going to the High School for Performing Arts. I'm going to succeed." Zarah stopped. Her voice had risen. She was almost shouting.

Quanamina was shaking her head as though she didn't understand a word Zarah had said.

"Don't you understand? I had to do it. It was the only way I could go there and serve even if they paid me. I played a maid as though I were on stage or in a movie. It was a theatrical performance. And I danced. I went there as an entertainer, not a servant."

Quanamina sighed and heaved herself out of the chair. She lit a candle and gave the lamp to Zarah.

"It was the only way I could do it," Zarah said, almost pleading.

"Go to bed, child."

Zarah took the lamp to her room. Shadows danced on the wall, growing, shrinking, mocking. She put on the long T-shirt she slept in and turned down the wick until the light was gone. Then she sat on the edge of her bed. She wasn't sleepy. She felt shaky inside, as though something important had just happened but she didn't know what.

TEN

~~~

IN THE morning Quanamina could hardly move. She sat on the stuffed blue sofa with her legs propped up. "I got misery in my legs," she told Zarah.

For breakfast they ate cold ham and biscuits left over from the party. Loomis fed some of the party scraps to the chickens.

"Give some to Frizzle," Zarah told Loomis. "He's free to find his own food but he likes treats, too."

Quanamina had Zarah bring her some honey and vinegar from the well house. "Now mix it good in a jar, half a cup of each." She waited in the rocking chair on the back porch, her feet propped on a barrel.

Zarah shook the jar vigorously until the thick dark honey had been lightened with the vinegar. Then Quanamina swallowed a teaspoon of it.

"Helps the misery," she said.

Next she had Zarah mix an egg, vinegar, and turpentine in another jar and shake it for several minutes.

"You're not going to drink that?" Zarah asked in horror, afraid that her grandmother would poison herself with home remedies.

Quanamina gave her a small smile. "Bring me a rag. I rub it on my leg."

"I'll do it," Zarah said. She dipped the rag into the cloudy yellow liquid and gently stroked her grandmother's veiny, knotted legs. It seemed to have a soothing effect. Quanamina leaned back and closed her eyes. She seemed to be asleep as Zarah tiptoed away.

But at noon she wasn't any better. She swallowed more of the honey concoction and put more of the egg remedy on her legs. "Sometime it take awhile," Quanamina said.

Zarah brought her some aspirin. "Try two of these." She got a glass of milk from the cooler. She always drank milk when her legs hurt from ballet.

"Thank you, child," Quanamina said.

"Why don't you lie down awhile?"

"Reckon I will. I be too old to work like I did last night."

"How old are you?" Zarah had wondered but hadn't dared to ask.

"I be born in the last century," was all she would say. If she had been born in 1899 she would be eighty-three now, Zarah figured. But she seemed older than eighty-three, especially today.

"Come on, Loomis, let's take a walk so Quanamina can sleep."

She picked up her snake stick from the back door where she kept it beside Loomis's broom. "Let's try this path," she said. "I haven't been to the heart of the island yet, only around the edges."

The woods were dense here and still. The river and ocean

breezes had to make their way through the thick foliage of oak and gum and cypress, the glossy leathery leaves of swamp magnolia starred with white flowers, the long dark green needles of pine. At a fork Zarah started to go to the left but Loomis stopped her.

"We go this way. We don't go that way."

"Why? What's that way?"

"The graveyard." His voice was so low she could hardly hear him. She hesitated a moment. She could always come back later. He looked relieved when she followed him to the right.

The path opened up to the marsh, the same one she had crossed on the footbridge when she first came to the island. The marsh seemed to have split the two islands, then drained into the creek where she had met Benicia.

The heat was intense. Sweat trickled all over Zarah. She was accustomed to sweat in ballet but just breathing made her sweat here. It felt like a million snakes crawling down her back, her legs, under her arms. She wiped her face with the back of her hand.

And the noise. The marsh noise was as loud as the traffic in New York, seething, whining, humming, droning, all of these and more. The marsh was alive. Things were happening there. Snakes were eating frogs, fish eating other fish, birds eating fish. And alligators were eating everything. Crabs ate the leftovers.

Zarah felt a shiver go up her back even in the hot sun. It was beautiful and terrible at the same time. Once there was only one island, she thought. Now there are two. Someday there won't be any. Quanamina had said that Domingo was forty acres at the time of the Civil War but now it was only thirty.

A small brown and white bird perched on a ribbon of marsh grass sang, *"Tsip-tsip-tsip-seeee-saaaaay."*

"What's that?" she asked Loomis.

"Bidi bidi."

At the sound of her voice the bird zipped across the marsh, skimming the top of the grass, then dropped out of sight. A hundred frogs hit the water with liquid plops.

A cardinal streaked by, a smear of red against the green. "What's that?"

"Bidi bidi."

So a bidi bidi was a small bird to Loomis, anything that wasn't a hu hu.

"The marshes sing," Loomis said. "But the ocean got teeth. It eat up the land. Someday eat it all up. Swallow it whole just like the whale eat Jonah. Then the ocean burp and there be another island."

Zarah looked at him. She'd never heard him talk so much. He was always so quiet, always watching her as though she was strange to him, from outer space somewhere. He didn't seem to understand her. But he knew the marsh as well as other children knew their ABC's. It was his world. "Hey, Loomis, you're a poet."

He grinned. She noticed that he had lost a tooth.

There was a splash nearby. Zarah's head jerked up. She was always on the alert for alligators. "What was that?"

"A kuta."

"What's a kuta?"

"Just a kuta."

Zarah stared at him. He didn't know how to tell her what a kuta was in English.

"Like that." He pointed to the green turtle watch on her left ankle.

"Oh. A turtle."

"Turkle," he said softly.

He noticed things and made connections. She bet he could learn if somebody taught him. "Would you like to learn a song, Loomis?"

He nodded.

"A-B-C-D-E-F-G," she sang.

He sang it with her. They went through it twice and then he sang it by himself. He learned fast. How had she thought he was retarded? Because he didn't know her language. Because he had lived in almost total isolation, away from other children of his age.

"That was very good," she told Loomis. "I think you have earned a reward." She took off the turtle watch and strapped it to his wrist.

"I'll teach you to tell time," she promised.

He looked at his wrist every few steps as they went back to the house.

Quanamina said she felt much better when she woke up that afternoon. "My remedies always work."

Zarah thought it was more likely the aspirin working. "Want to hear a song?" she asked. "Sing our song for Quanamina," she told Loomis.

He sang the ABC song for her and then sang it again.

"Zarah learn me," he said.

"Zarah taught me," she said.

"Taught." He held out his arm. "She gimme this kuta watch. Turkle," he corrected himself.

"That good, Loomis. You sing real smart." Quanamina wiped her eyes with the edge of her hem. "Turpentine burn my eye," she said.

ELEVEN

~~~~~~

ZARAH stayed away from the beach after the party. She never wanted to see Benicia again. She tried to exercise on the river beach but it sloped and the sand wasn't as good for her feet. Next she tried the porch but the floor was uneven. After two days without exercising she went back to her palm root *barre*. She was doing *pliés* when she felt someone watching her. Out of the corner of her eye she saw Benicia sitting on the palm log across the creek. She went on with her exercises.

When she finished she turned to go without speaking. She heard splashing in the creek. Zarah walked faster.

"Hey, wait up," Benicia called. "You can't just walk off like that. I've been here every day waiting for you. I wasn't going to come today but I saw you from the attic window. Just like the ghost," she trailed off.

Did she think they could go on being friends after what had happened? Zarah turned around and yelled at her. "You can't tell me what to do. I'm not one of the Saylor slaves."

Benicia stopped and backed into the middle of the stream. "What are you talking about?"

"I'm talking about being invited to a party and then having to serve at it. Mo biscuits, Miss Benicia?" she said in her Butterfly McQueen voice.

Benicia looked down at her bare feet. "I didn't have anything to do with that."

Zarah walked away.

"Wait, Zarah, let me explain."

Zarah whirled, fists on hips, and faced her. "You don't have to explain why I couldn't come to your white bread party. It's because I'm Afro-American. Black. Colored. Negro. Blackbird. Coon. Spade. Nigra. Nigger. Niggerniggernigger." The words tasted like dirt.

Benicia looked as though Zarah had slapped her. A dark red stain moved up from her neck. Her eyes looked red, too, as though she had been crying, but now she was angry, too. "You're using those words, not me. I've never used them in my life." She was shouting now. "I invited you to my party. I didn't have anything to do with your serving."

"Well, your grandmother then. Mrs. Saylor of Saylor's Landing who can't give up that glorious time of magnolias and cavaliers." Her voice dripped with Elizabeth Taylor sarcasm.

"It's true," Benicia admitted, "my grandmother is like that. She did want you to serve. We had a big fight about it. I told her I'd invited you as my friend. I told her that we aren't like that where I live in California. She cried and said that wasn't her world. I said it was time her world started changing. She finally said all right, since I had already invited you. But then your grandmother said you would come and serve. It was your grandmother, not mine. My grandmother thought you needed the money." She stopped. Now she really looked about to cry.

Zarah stared at her. "Quanamina said I would serve? Quanamina?"

"That's right."

"I don't believe you."

"It's true. Ask her."

"I will."

Zarah ran down the beach. Her ears rang with Benicia's words. Her own grandmother. She could hear Benicia calling behind her. "Wait, Zarah. Come back." The words grew fainter as she reached the path.

She tore up the path, forgetting about snakes and alligators and even chiggers. She didn't feel the branches ripping her hair. She'd left her sneakers on the beach. She didn't even notice the sharp sticks that struck her feet.

Quanamina was stirring a pot of soup in the cookshed when Zarah arrived out of breath. She stood in the open doorway panting.

"What the matter, child. You see a ghost?"

Words fell out of Zarah's mouth like stones. "Quanamina, why did you make me serve at that party?"

When Quanamina didn't answer, Zarah said, "Benicia told me. I was invited as a guest."

Quanamina didn't turn around. She went on stirring. "It wasn't fitten. Them not our ways."

"They are my ways. I don't belong to this nowhere place. I live in the real world. Out there." She spread her hands. "I'm going to be famous someday. People will know my name in London. In Paris. In Tokyo. You don't even know where those places are. You don't even care."

"They far away from Domingo?"

"Yes, a long way. In time and distance."

"Then what do they matter here?"

"They matter to me. I matter to me. You shamed me, Quanamina."

Now Quanamina looked at Zarah. The whites of her eyes seemed yellow in the dim light of the cookshed. She looked old and tired. "How I shame you when you shame me?"

"Because I am not a servant and never have been and never will be."

"Nothing wrong with honest work."

"No, there isn't. But I wasn't asked to serve. I was asked to come as a guest. As Benicia's friend."

"Miz Saylor don't want this."

"No, she didn't." Zarah took a deep breath. "But since Benicia had invited me, she accepted it." Zarah didn't say that it was time for Mrs. Saylor's world to change, too.

Quanamina went on stirring the pot, her body moving in rhythm with the spoon. Then she said, "Hand me that jar on the shelf by you, green one there."

Zarah found the jar. Quanamina left the spoon in the pot while she tried to unscrew the jar lid. Her hands seemed stiff and awkward.

"Here, I'll do it." Zarah was impatient.

Quanamina put some leaves in the pot.

"You need a cool drink of water," she said. "You need to cool off. You all hot from running."

Zarah didn't want to cool off. She wanted Quanamina to see her anger. It went all the way to the bone.

"Let's go in the house." Zarah followed her to the sitting room. Quanamina opened her Bible. "My eyes bad. Read Jeremiah 2:36."

With a sigh Zarah took the big heavy Bible off Quanamina's lap and flipped through the pages until she found the verse. "Why gaddest thou about so much to change thy way? Thou also shalt be ashamed of Egypt as thou wast ashamed of Assyria.

"What's that supposed to mean?"

Quanamina pursed her lips and didn't answer.

"No," Zarah said. "I won't be ashamed of Egypt. I'll dance there. The president will invite me to the palace. They'll have a great reception in my honor. But even if they don't, I will know I am a dancer and that I did what I had come there to do."

There was another long silence. Then Quanamina said, "I wash and iron your dress. It hang in your room. I was saving that white piqué for my funeral dress."

"You can make another one," Zarah told her. "I'll send you some more piqué when I get back to New York."

Slowly Quanamina shook her head. "I ruin my eyes on that dress. Can't sew no more. No more time left."

"There's plenty of time." Her grandmother just didn't understand. "Why can't you understand that I don't have to be a servant? I can be a doctor or a lawyer or a dancer. Maybe even president. I can be anything I want to be. All I have to do is plan and work hard."

Quanamina shook her head again. "I work hard all my life. Henry work hard. We had ten babies. All dead. You and Loomis and this island all I got left. I got to take care of you. Teach you how to live in this world."

"I know how to live. I can take care of myself. I live in New York City. You have to be able to take care of yourself there." Now Zarah understood why Quanamina never asked her questions about her life. She didn't know anything about life away from these three islands, Domingo, Saylor, and Barnett. She didn't know what to ask.

"This my land," Quanamina said. "Don't do nothin' to lose it. Don't make the white folks mad."

"Don't what?" Zarah wasn't sure she had heard right.

"Don't make the white folks mad."

"Why? What's wrong with making white folks mad?"

"Maybe take my island."

"They can't take your island if you own it."

Quanamina didn't answer.

"You own it, don't you?"

"In there." Quanamina pointed at the Bible. "There a paper in there say Domingo belong to Quanamina Brown."

"You mean a deed?"

Quanamina nodded.

Zarah found the deed. It was old and yellow. "Here it is. So why are you worried about making whites mad and losing the island?"

Quanamina's eyes darted around the room. "Tax money," she whispered.

"What do you mean, tax money? You pay your taxes, don't you?"

"Not this year. Ain't got money this year."

"What are you going to do?"

"Trust in the Lord and hope. Ain't nothing else I can do."

"That's not enough. You can have the money Mrs. Saylor paid me. And I've got some left from my trip down. That's probably over twenty dollars. Will that help?"

Quanamina shook her head. "It help some. But it ain't enough. If I can get rid of the misery in my hand, I can make baskets to sell. We be all right then. We be like we always been."

She went back to the cookshed. Zarah sat listening to the popping of the tin roof. It was only midmorning and already the roof was ticking and snapping in the heat like it was midafternoon. Sometimes it even sounded like someone was walking over it.

Zarah thought about her grandmother. Quanamina believed if she could keep everything the same in her world, it would stay the same and her island would be safe. The smallest change could wreck everything. That was why she had made her granddaughter serve at the party. It had always been that way here.

TWELVE

~~~

THE POSTCARD had been folded in the middle, dog-eared, and dented. The St. Louis Arch soared by the Mississippi River. A crack ran through the river, ending in a small tear at the bottom of the card.

Hi, Chicken, How are you enjoying the island? I bet you're eating a lot. We met a man who knows important people at Motown. Big stuff, Baby. We're heading up there when we finish this gig. Wish me luck. Give my regards to your grandmother. Love, Ila.

Zarah read it through again. It was postmarked Kansas City, July 24, almost a week ago. She'd been here almost six weeks now. School would be starting in a little over a month. She had to get home.

Zarah read the card again. Then she crossed the rickety

footbridge and went up the camel bridge over the Culebra River. She stood on the hump of the bridge and looked down. The water was bright blue today, reflecting the deep blue sky. Barnett Island shimmered on the horizon. At the edge of the river fiddler crabs scurried sideways in the marsh mud. They made clicking sounds and the mud seemed to tick. A handful of blue butterflies, like bits of the sky, drifted across the marsh.

Zarah tore the postcard into as many tiny pieces as she could. Then she threw them into the river. She watched as the bits floated until they became indistinguishable from the spots of sunlight on the surface of the water.

The tide was coming in. Every twelve hours it came in. Every twelve hours it went out, varying only a few minutes each time. No one needed clocks on Domingo. High and low tide. Night and day. That was all anyone needed to know. No need for calendars either. Summer or winter. Cold or hot. Nothing made much difference. Nothing but black and white. Past and future. But these people didn't even know there was a future. And they seemed to think that only white mattered, that they couldn't be dancers and doctors or anything but what they'd always been.

Around the bend Quanamina and Loomis were crabbing. Not for fiddlers but for real crabs. Zarah had taken one look at the first one Loomis caught, and left. They were horrible things with those ugly claws and mean eyes. She left the bridge and walked back to the house but turned off before she got there. She wanted to see the cemetery.

The ground rose slightly as the track curved around an enormous live oak dripping with moss. The sun was shut out suddenly as Zarah entered a grove of cedars almost as big as the oak. Their foliage seemed to soak up the light. The graves lay haphazardly in the sandy soil. Some were outlined by bricks. Several were coated with a slab of cracked cement. Some were just sunken places in the dirt. It was cool under the cedars away from the sun. Zarah shivered.

The air was still, as though it were holding its breath. Zarah stood in the middle of the graves and listened. The island seemed to enter her pores and breathe with her. There was a tingling down her spine and on her fingertips. She felt a mystical connection to these people. They were her ancestors. Their bones were under the ground in graves that were over a hundred years old, some of them, maybe two hundred years. Quanamina had told her that first it was the cemetery for the Saylor slaves. Then it became the burying ground for her family when they took over Domingo.

Except for Ila, Zarah hadn't seen any of her relatives until she came to the island, not since her father died. Ila's brother Roy had come to the funeral but he was off in the army somewhere and she'd never seen him again.

Zarah traced some of the inscriptions on the cement-covered graves. "In memory of Shakirah born a slave died 1899 at rest." Her grandfather Henry had put down the cement.

"He done all our children," Quanamina had said, "the ones here." A daughter had died in Detroit, Zarah's father in New Jersey. Both were buried far away from Domingo.

Henry's grave had a rusty oil lantern at the head. At the foot was a rusty hammer, saw, and shovel. A broken cup lay in the middle beside a strangely twisted root that had turned gray with weathering and had fine hairline splits all over it. Some of the other graves had things on them, too, cracked cups, odd roots, a broken oar, rusty clocks.

Zarah counted the children's graves, eight of them, Rosa, Boston, Henry, Edward, George, Osman, Charles, Sam. Most had died before the age of four. The last three had drowned in the hurricane of 1944. "My little baby angels," Quanamina had called them. Only two of the ten children born to Quanamina and Henry Brown had grown up and had children. Then they had died, too. Children didn't die like that anymore. Zarah wondered what had been wrong with so many of them.

She wondered why Loomis was so afraid of the cemetery. Because of the children's graves, she guessed. But she wasn't afraid. The cemetery was peaceful to her. She turned back to the path. As she reached the fork in the path a man appeared out of nowhere. Zarah almost screamed aloud.

"Are you Miz Brown's girl?"

Zarah nodded. He was a pale white man with yellow hair under a straw Panama hat and a yellow moustache under a red nose. He wore cream trousers, a white short-sleeved shirt, and a cream and white striped tie.

"I went up to the house and knocked, front and back. Nobody was home. Listen, you tell Miz Brown that $250,000 is my last offer. She can keep the acre with her house and the graveyard on it and right of way. We can buy this place for back taxes if she don't sell." He took a card out of his wallet and wrote on it with a gold ballpoint. "This is my home phone number. Tell her to call me when she's ready to sell. Call anytime, day or night."

Zarah took the card. Shelby James Cosgrove, Attorney at Law, she read. She put it in her pocket. "Yessir, I tell her."

He fanned himself with the hat. "It sure is hot out here away from the sea breeze." He pointed the hat at her. "This is our last offer. You tell her now."

~~~~~~~~~~

ZARAH found Quanamina and Loomis in the living room. The shades were pulled down. Quanamina had her Bible open on her lap. Loomis was on the floor beside her playing with his battered teddy bear.

"He gone?" Quanamina asked.

"Yes. He's gone. Why don't you sell the island? It would solve all of your problems. That man said he'd give you $250,000 for it. That's a lot of money. You could go on living here. But then you'd have money for things. You could have electricity. And clothes. And Loomis could have books and toys."

"Don't need them things. This island more than dirt. It been good to my people. Feed us, good time and bad. My ancestor bone in it."

. "But, Quanamina, you could still have the part of the island you live on and the part your ancestors are buried in."

"No. My daddy and Henry and their daddy all work this land. Got to protect it from developers. They ruin it. This land good to us. We always farm for food. Get oysters till they go bracky. Then we still eat them. Fish, crab, shrimp. We keep hog, chicken. It a good life. Got to keep it for Loomis. He be safe here. It a good place."

But not so good for babies, Zarah thought, remembering all the little graves she had seen.

"Don't want to talk about it no more," Quanamina said. "Loomis and me, we go back to our crabbing."

Zarah stayed on the screened porch and thought about the island. It was worth more money than she had ever dreamed of. If the island were hers, she would sell it in a minute. Why would anybody want to live like this if they didn't have to?

Quanamina cooked devil crab cakes that night. Ila had been right about one thing, Zarah thought when she bit into the crisp tangy cake with the flakey white crab inside. She was eating well.

After supper Quanamina said, "It rain tonight."

The sky had been clear all day with only high streamers of clouds. "How can you tell?"

"Smell the air. It smell fresh. An' my misery bother me."

The air on Domingo always smelled fresh to Zarah unless she was close to the marsh. She put a tape of gospel music on her player.

"That nice music," Quanamina said as she settled down in the green chair. Loomis was looking at the pictures in Zarah's June issue of Vogue. She had missed the July issue.

"I'll leave it for you when I go home," Zarah said. But after the postcard today, she didn't think it would be soon.

When Loomis went to bed, she asked Quanamina about the things she had seen on the graves.

"Them thing to help in the next world," she said.

"What about the funny roots?"

"Charm root. To help the dead. Bring them good luck."

Zarah thought about that for awhile. It was like rabbit's feet for the dead. Or lighting candles.

"If all your children but two, my daddy and Lena, died when they were babies, who is Loomis? He's not Lena's son, is he?"

"No, he Lena grandson. Lena the one died in Detroit. Ercelline, Lena daughter."

So Quanamina was Loomis's great-grandmother. "Did she die, too?"

"No. Ercelline come here when Loomis just born. 'I brung you my angel baby to see,' she tell me, 'to make up for the ones you lost.' Next day, she gone. She sometime send Loomis a card, a little money, a toy. Last year she send him a sweater. It so small it fit a baby. She forgot he grow."

"Where do the things come from?"

"I don't know. It hard to make out letters."

Now Zarah knew why her grandmother hadn't known she was coming. She couldn't read very well, maybe not at all. "Didn't she ever come back to see Loomis?"

"No, she like her daddy people. Jenkins never were reliable. They from 'round Charleston."

Later, when Zarah was in bed, the rain came just as Quanamina said it would. She lay listening to it. The drops sounded like bullets on the tin roof. The noise was deafening. She couldn't have heard a jet if one had buzzed the house. But it was an oddly comforting, lulling sound.

THIRTEEN

~~~~~~~~~~

A STRONG wind blew in with the rain during the night. The next morning Zarah found the dishpan in the yard. The baskets had disappeared off the porch. Loomis's broom was at the bottom of the steps. The frizzle chicken was fussing at it when she went down to pick up the dishpan.

"Keep your feathers on," she told the chicken. At the sound of her voice it ran under the steps and fussed at her from safety, its feathers bouncing and jerking with every squawk.

Loomis went to work on the yard. Zarah helped him pick up the sticks and limbs that had fallen. He was raking energetically when she went to the beach.

The palm tree she had been using as a *barre* was gone. She walked up the beach to see if it had been washed ashore but she couldn't find it. It must have washed out and sunk or maybe floated away. Maybe it was on its way to Africa or South America or New York. The beach was littered with seaweed, shells, cigarette butts, plastic trash, lumber, palm fronds, seeds, bottles, Styrofoam floats, bits of rope. She saw a red sneaker, a child's sandpail, the lid of a Styrofoam cooler, and a rubber ball. She put the ball in her pocket for Loomis. It was red with blue stars on it. Maybe he could teach the frizzle chicken to fetch. The bird seemed to like him. It often followed him around as he raked.

She went back down the beach to the stream and stood letting the water tickle her toes as it ran into the sea. She should go see Benicia. What happened wasn't her fault. She was caught up in the island ways, too. Zarah walked south down the beach toward the road to the Saylors' house.

Benicia met her halfway. She looked wary, as though she thought Zarah might yell at her again. "I'm looking for a lost palm tree," Zarah said. "You didn't happen to see it come this way, did you? It was wearing a red collar with a tag that said 'Rover.' "

Benicia laughed. "I saw you from the window. I didn't think you were coming when you went the other way."

"I guess the storm washed my tree out to sea. Poor tree. It was a good *barre*. It seemed to be firmly planted in the sand."

"The sea is very powerful," Benicia said. "My grandmother told me that houses get washed away sometimes after big storms. That's why the island people don't build on the ocean side. Only outsiders think the nice pretty ocean won't get them. My grandmother knows a woman who lived across the street from a beach house. After a storm she had the whole beach house in her living room."

They looked at the ocean as its waves endlessly broke and foamed against the sand. Then Zarah said, "I almost didn't come this way. I stood in the stream and thought about it for awhile. But then I decided to come."

"I'm glad you did. My grandparents are nice to me and everything but they are so different. They want me to sit around and read and be ladylike. I don't have anybody to talk to but that drip Mary Saylor."

Zarah looked down at the tangle of shells and seaweed dragged up by the waves. She had to do it. She owed it to Benicia, who was caught between the past and present with her grandparents, too.

"I came to apologize for yelling at you."

"It's OK. I understand."

"I guess I do, too, now. I had a talk with my grandmother," Zarah said. She picked up a bit of shiny green shell but it was only beach glass worn by the waves. She tossed it at the waves. It fell in the water with a gulping sound. "I guess it's hard being old. My grandmother is afraid of change, any kind of change. She doesn't understand anything different and she's scared. She thinks she'll lose everything if anything changes."

Benicia chunked a shell. It skittered across the top of a wave before the water curled over on it. "I think my grandmother is the same way."

"I like changes. I hope I never get that way."

"Me, too," Benicia said. She shaded her eyes and scanned the beach ahead of them. "There aren't any palm trees on Saylor, but I saw some other trees you might be able to use for a *barre*. Want to take a look?"

They found some parts of dead trees, possibly oak, Benicia said, that Zarah could use. They were bleached white as bones but seemed sturdy enough.

"I'm tired of watching," Benicia said as Zarah bent her knees in a *demi-plié*. "Why don't you teach me how to do it, too. Then we can do it together."

"OK. I taught the little kids sometimes when the teacher was on the phone or had to do something in my first ballet school."

"How'd you get into ballet anyway?" Benicia asked after she had groaned her way through warm-up stretching.

"It was after my father was killed when I was six. That first Christmas was awful. We went to see *The Nutcracker* at The American Ballet." It had been the worst Christmas of Zarah's life. Londra had insisted on taking them to the ballet. Ila hadn't wanted to go and because of that Zarah hadn't wanted to go either. But Londra made them go. Zarah remembered crying while Londra buttoned her coat and getting sick in the taxi and stopping for a Coke to settle her stomach. Then Zarah had fallen under the spell of the ballet, the music, the costumes, the sets, the dancers. It had been magic. The ballet had made Zarah happy, made her forget for a time, her sadness and her mother's depression. Now when she danced, she always felt the happiness of that day.

"When I went home I danced all over the place. Londra insisted that I have lessons. And that was the beginning of my career."

"It sounds like a fairy tale," Benicia said.

Zarah laughed. "Not quite. There's been plenty of hard work, sweat, blood, and blisters. One year I was too tall to fit into the costumes. My class was doing the marshmallow babies that year. They got to roll around on stage and be cute. All I got to do was stand around in a makeshift Arabian attendant costume. I wouldn't drink milk for a month because

I didn't want to grow. My mother told my teacher. He said my bones would get soft if I didn't drink my milk."

"It must have been fun to be in *The Nutcracker*. I went to see it once in San Francisco," Benicia said.

"It is. After you learn a few steps, I'll teach you a little dance to the Russian dance from *The Nutcracker*."

"Terrific."

"OK, this is first position. Put your heels together and make your feet go straight out."

Benicia tried it. "Ouch! That hurts."

"You can't just turn your feet out. You have to start with the hips, then the knees, and the feet will follow."

"Not mine." Benicia struggled to turn her feet out.

"It will come. Don't push it. Let your bones get used to it gradually. Is that better?"

"Not much."

"Now bend your knees a little."

Benicia held onto the tree and bent her knees.

"That was a *demi-plié*," Zarah told her. "It will make you sore because you're using muscles you've probably not used much. But it's good for you."

Benicia groaned. "Like taking medicine. Because it's good for you," she mimicked Zarah.

But it was worth it, she said, when she started learning the steps to the Russian dance.

~~~~~~~~~

MAKE a C like you're going to make a circle, Loomis, only don't go all the way around."

Loomis took the stick he was using to write in the dirt.

He did it again. This time he only went three-quarters of the way around. "You're getting it!" Zarah told him. She was teaching him to write his ABC's while Quanamina watched from her rocking chair on the porch. Loomis was learning fast.

"I bet you could learn to read," she told him after he had learned D, E, and F. She turned to Quanamina. "He needs some books."

"Don't have any," she said, "except the Bible. That too hard." She frowned.

"But he needs books to help him learn," Zarah said. "Aren't there any libraries around here?"

"Don't know about libraries."

"Loomis is a fast learner but he needs things. If you sold the island you could buy books for him."

Quanamina didn't say anything, just went on rocking. She had leaves sticking out of her dress. "Oily leaves," she said when Zarah asked her what they were. "Bring down fever."

Zarah had never heard of such things but Quanamina swore that the leaves helped. "Shouldn't you go to a doctor?"

"Doctors cost money," Quanamina said. "Don't need them. Got all the remedy I need here." She waved her arm at the woods. She was taking her vinegar and honey concoction again and rubbing the turpentine mixture on her legs. But Zarah didn't think any of the remedies were helping. Quanamina always seemed tired. She was taking aspirin daily now. Benicia had given Zarah several bottles. Zarah worried about how many Quanamina was taking. She had warned her grandmother about taking too many and read the instructions on the bottle aloud, but she didn't know if Quanamina was following them.

The days seemed to grow hotter. Now they did everything but sleep on the two porches. Zarah was willing to do that but Quanamina wouldn't let her. "Best be inside at night," she said. She didn't mention spirits again but Zarah thought that was the reason for sleeping in the stifling house.

One hot day when the morning glories hung their heads over the back porch railing and even the frizzle chicken seemed to pant with the heat, Quanamina stayed in bed. "I can't seem to get up this morning," she said when Loomis brought Zarah in to check on her.

"Stay in bed and rest," Zarah said. "I'll take care of everything. I cook at home."

Zarah was good at opening cans and pushing buttons on the microwave. But here the stove was heated with wood and there were few cans. Loomis told her how to put the firewood in the stove with twists of paper to start the fire. Zarah didn't want to admit it to anybody, not even herself, but she was a little afraid of the stove. The fire made a roaring sound when she opened the door and reminded her of Hansel and Gretel. She told the story to Loomis as she opened cans and found pots. "And then Hansel pushed the witch into the stove."

"An' she burn up?"

"Yep. That's what happened."

"All the way up?"

"All the way."

"They eat the candy house?"

Zarah couldn't remember the rest of the story. "Um, they went to live with their cousins and whenever they got hungry for candy, they would come back and eat a little more of the house."

"They eat the house up?"

"No." Zarah poured grits into a bowl. "Every time they ate part of the house, it would grow back."

Loomis smiled at that. But he didn't smile at the lumpy grits or the burned bacon. "You got to stir the pot," Quanamina told her when she saw the grits. "And put some butter in them."

At lunchtime Zarah decided to cook noodles. Nobody could go wrong with noodles. But Loomis was suspicious of her cooking now.

"What that is?"

Zarah started to say buttered noodles. "Worms," she said.

"Worms!"

"Sure. Didn't you ever eat worms?"

"Naw. They ain't worms."

"Sure they are."

"Crawly worms?"

"If I hadn't cooked them, they'd be crawling all over your plate."

Loomis grinned and picked up his spoon. He tasted the noodles. "Them ain't worm. Is they?"

~~~~~~~~

SOON Zarah was doing most of the cooking, even when Quanamina was able to get out of bed. She was dizzy and couldn't stand on her feet long. But with her direction, Zarah's meals improved. She learned to stir the grits and to make soup with fresh vegetables from the garden, simmered on the warm stove all day and eaten with corn bread or biscuits. Once when Quanamina was feeling better she went down to the river and fished with Loomis. Zarah made smutter fish and it was almost as good as Quanamina's. Only a little of it burned around the edges.

One day Quanamina was so listless that Zarah fed her cold vegetable soup with a spoon. "You getting to be a good cook," Quanamina said with a smile. "Good thing you come so I can teach you." Soup dribbled down her chin and she didn't even try to wipe it off. Zarah did it for her and tried to hide her alarm. She had never seen an adult who couldn't sit up and eat. But with the evening cool, Quanamina insisted on helping with supper.

At night they listened to Zarah's tapes. Sometimes Quanamina told stories about the family. "Henry farm, grow cotton till the boll weevil come in and eat the cotton, bite it all up, rot it all up, it all die. Do a little lumbering till the trees all gone. He do a little oystering. The oyster bed go all bracky and die. Henry say it time for him to die, too. But he fish a little, grow a little crop, keep pig, cow, chicken. We get by."

Sometimes she talked about her children, her angels. "They always with me, every day of my life. I be with them soon." She talked about the flood that followed the hurricane in 1944. "Water come right up over the island. Hundred people die on Saylor, on Domingo, on Daufuskie, on Hilton Head, all the coast islands. And all my sweet little baby angels."

Zarah asked her about Osman. "Why did you name him that?"

"Zalinda was very beautiful. When slave catchers go to her village they take her back to pens. Osman see her. He want her but she sent away in a slave ship. Her daughter Shakirah, Osman daughter. One day man wash up on beach.

Zalinda say it him. He come looking for her. They bury him in the graveyard."

Her words were music in the darkness.

Sometimes she told Zarah stories about her daddy when he was a boy. "You daddy had him a goat name of Pony. Fix him a little cart out of this and that. Used to drive Pony over to Saylors'. Sell little pies I fry to the workers, nickel a pie. Took in his head he would plow Pony. Pony didn't 'gree. Willie make him a plow, hitch up Pony. That goat just balk and balk right there in the patch. Then he back up, he go sideways, anyways but front ways. That goat ain't no pony. You daddy change his name to Mule cause he just as stubborn. Mule chew through the pen one night. Maybe he swim away to Saylor. Maybe gator got him. Never see him again.

"You daddy was a smart boy. He always trying things. He try to train a pig to pull the cart. Pig just sit down and look at you daddy. He ain't pull no cart. Pig got more patience than you daddy. He outlook him. You daddy make a little basket he hang from a stick over his shoulder to sell pie from. He never did plow that patch. Have to turn it with a shovel."

She was silent, remembering. Then she said, "You a lot like you daddy."

Zarah felt sudden tears. She had never expected Quanamina to say that. "How? How am I like him?"

"Always doing things different."

Zarah wanted to ask more but Loomis had fallen asleep while Quanamina was talking. Zarah carried him to his bed but Quanamina stayed in her chair. When Zarah came back she said, "You good with Loomis. You take care of him."

"He's very smart."

"You teach him, take care of him when I'm gone."

"He'll be grown up by then," Zarah said but Quanamina interrupted her.

"When I be gone, you look in my Bible. Now read to me. I can't read so good now."

Zarah read for a long time from Revelations. It was late when Quanamina told her to stop. Then she asked for one more verse.

"And I saw a new heaven and a new earth: for the first heaven and the first earth were passed away and there was no more sea."

"It time to sleep now," Quanamina said.

FOURTEEN

~~~~~~~

THE OWL was enormous. It opened its huge mouth. Angels flew out like a swarm of white butterflies. "Hu hu," they cried in ghostly voices. Zarah floated up to the door of the owl.

"Zarah, Zarah, wake up," said a voice. Zarah opened her eyes. Loomis was shaking her shoulder.

"What's the matter?"

"It Quanamina. She won't get up."

"What time is it?" she started to say, then remembered. It was daytime. The hour didn't matter. But she could tell it was early. The sun threw fresh shadows across the dirt yard outside her window.

"She's probably still tired," she told Loomis. "Go back to sleep or go out and play or something." She turned over and buried her face in her pillow. She liked dark rooms. She would never get back to sleep now.

"She cold," Loomis persisted. "I put a quilt over her but she still cold."

"Did she say she was cold?"

"She didn't say nothing."

Zarah sat up. "OK, Loomis, wait out on the porch."

It didn't mean anything, she told herself as she walked barefoot over the bare floor to Quanamina's room. Old people got cold sometimes, even when it was warm and muggy, especially people with arthritis or rheumatism or whatever Quanamina had.

Zarah went in her grandmother's room and closed the door behind her. Quanamina was on her back in the double bed, the white sheet pulled up to her chin. A blue flowered quilt lay in awkward folds over her. Her hair was in two neat braids on her shoulders. Her face was smooth. She looked asleep. Zarah touched her arm. It was cold.

"Quanamina?" she spoke softly.

There was no answer.

She shook her grandmother's arm but Quanamina didn't move.

Zarah took a hand mirror from her grandmother's dresser and held it under Quanamina's nose, the way she had seen people do on TV. She held it there for a long time but no cloud appeared on its surface. She rubbed it on her T-shirt and held it under her grandmother's nose again. But the mirror's surface remained clear and unclouded.

She was dead. Zarah had never seen a dead person before. Her father's casket had been closed. Ila had wanted to remember him the way he was the last time she saw him, when he was alive. Quanamina didn't look dead. She looked like she was sleeping and might wake up any minute and ask Zarah what she was standing there gawking at.

No, she thought. She can't be dead. She almost said it aloud but she remembered Loomis out on the porch. She didn't want to upset him. Not yet.

Quanamina must have died in her sleep. Everybody always said it was the best way to die, without pain or fear. That's what people always said. "That's how I want to go."

But not yet. Not before she knew that Zarah wasn't shameful. Now Zarah would never have a chance to show her that she wasn't a disgrace.

Now she could never tell Quanamina that she loved her. Zarah felt her own skin grow cold. Never never never. There was an awful finality to it.

She took her grandmother's cold hand and held it. The hand would never feel pain again but it would never do the tasks that gave her grandmother pleasure either—sewing, cooking, fishing, weaving baskets, soothing Loomis, cleaning Zarah's scraped knees.

Images crowded in on Zarah. Quanamina smoothing the folds of the peignoir, dressed for church, the roses bobbing on her hat, wearing an apron in the Saylors' kitchen. She brushed them aside. There was no time for that now. She had to think. Ila was out on the road with the Maroons. Zarah didn't even know what state they were in. There was no way to get in touch with them. Or with Londra. Londra was in California but Zarah didn't know where.

Quanamina's Bible was on the bed beside her. Zarah remembered her grandmother's words the night before. She picked up the heavy book. It fell open to the middle where a long envelope marked the place in Revelations she'd read from. Zarah opened the envelope.

It was a will, dated a week after Benicia's party, witnessed by William and Eleanor Saylor, signed by Quanamina Brown in crude letters, the shiny embossed gold seal of South Carolina at the end. Zarah scanned the one-page document. Quanamina had left Domingo to her and Loomis.

Zarah stared at the will. The island was theirs now but what good was it to them? Her thoughts raced ahead. They couldn't stay here and live the way Quanamina did. The welfare people might come and get her and Loomis. Put them in an orphanage or a shelter or a foster home somewhere. She didn't have any money to pay the taxes on Domingo either. Shelby Cosgrove would get the island whether she stayed here or went back to New York. Anyway she didn't have enough money to go to New York. And even if she did, there was Loomis. She would have to take him, too.

Zarah read the will again, more closely this time. ". . . to my beloved grandchildren," the will read. Not Zarah and my beloved Loomis but beloved grandchildren. Had Quanamina meant that or was it just lawyer talk?

She read on. "I know that my granddaughter Sarah Jane Brown, also known as Princess Zarah, will take care of Loomis Jackson."

Quanamina had called Zarah princess. Did that mean she accepted Zarah and her ways, approved of her? Zarah noticed a tear in her fingernail. She bit it while she tried to think what to do.

She had to go back to New York. Loomis, too. There was no question of staying here. All the money she had was maybe enough to get them to Charleston. If only Quanamina had sold the island. Now it couldn't be sold until she and Loomis were older, probably twenty-one. But they needed money now. By then there might not even be any island to sell if the sea kept eating it up. And the taxes.

Zarah looked at her grandmother. Her face was peaceful. The pain lines had been smoothed away by sleep and death. Quanamina entrusted Loomis and Domingo to her. She couldn't save both. She had to make a choice. She would have to try to sell Domingo.

Nobody knew Quanamina had died, not even Loomis. If she called the lawyer and got him to buy the island right now, this morning, she could sign Quanamina's name to the bill of sale. There must be a way to do it without him knowing Quanamina was dead.

She would work out the details later. First, she had to call the lawyer.

Zarah touched Quanamina's hand and felt a connection to her grandmother's bone and skin and blood, a connection to the past, to Shakirah and the baby angels and the others in the graveyard, and to the ones in Africa and other places, the others she had never even heard about. They all came together here on Domingo in her grandmother's hand. It was hypnotic to think of all those people, like reading the begats in the Bible. Zarah gave herself a little shake.

Now she had to deal with the present. Zarah stood up. "I'll do what I have to," she said softly to Quanamina.

She closed the bedroom door behind her and went out to find Loomis. He was sitting on the steps tossing corn kernels to the frizzle chicken.

"She all right?" There were worry lines across his forehead.

"She's sleeping." Zarah thought fast. She had to get to a telephone. It was too early to go to the Saylors'. They might listen. If they guessed what she was doing, they would stop her. She would have to go to Barnett to use the pay phone outside the store there. She went back to her room and got some change for the phone and the lawyer's card. She dressed and put on her sneakers. Then she dug in the dresser drawers until she found a pair of orange gloves. She stuffed them into her pocket.

"I've got to get some medicine," she told Loomis. She gave him a biscuit from the refrigerator and spooned syrup on it. She poured him a glass of milk from the cooler and drank a small glass herself. She didn't feel like eating anything.

"You stay here now and sweep the yard. OK?"

He nodded as she wiped his milk moustache off.

"I'll be back as soon as I can. Don't bother Quanamina. Let her sleep."

Zarah took the paddle off the nails where it hung over the door and went down the path to the river.

The boat was still there, the one she'd seen the day they went to church. Zarah turned it over easily. She untied the rope from the tree and stepped in. The boat wobbled horribly. It was almost a canoe, not nearly as sturdy as Junior's boat. Her knees turned to jelly. She got out of the boat.

"I can't do this," she said. A kingfisher flew out of a tree and a bird laughed somewhere behind her. She couldn't possibly paddle that tiny little boat across to Barnett. But there was no other way. She shaded her eyes and looked across at the low-lying island.

The boat would have to do. She hoped it wouldn't sink. Zarah got in again and sat down. She put on the orange gloves to protect her hands and picked up the paddle. Her palms were already sweating.

The river was pale blue and as smooth as a satin sheet. It slurped at the soft brown sand of the bank. Zarah thought the time must be around 6:30. She had forgotten to look at one of her watches. She pushed the boat away from the shore. It glided a few yards, then drifted into the river. There didn't seem to be any tidal current. Zarah thought it might be slack water, the twenty minutes or so between tides when the water seemed to stand still and catch its breath. She would have to hurry. If the tide turned it would flow away from Barnett and she would never be able to paddle against it.

She decided to head straight across the channel, then hug the marshes on the other side all the way to Barnett. She dipped the paddle into the water. Zarah felt the milk she'd drunk earlier lurch in her stomach. She was out in a river with unknown currents and creatures that had horrible claws and teeth and things she didn't want to think about. She concentrated on making the boat go where she wanted it to. It was harder than she had thought it would be. She dipped the paddle into the water and pulled it back on the right. The boat turned to the right. She dipped the paddle in again, this time on the left. The boat turned to the left, away from the course to Barnett.

Sweat dripped between her shoulder blades, down her sides. Zarah wiped her forehead with the back of her hand. The orange gloves were soaked. She would never get across if the boat zigzagged all the way. She would have to make it go straight. Zarah dipped the paddle on the other side. The boat went to the right but straighter this time. She paddled left, right. The zigzag course began to straighten with each pull of the paddle. She felt a rhythm in the thrust of the paddle and the glide of the boat. Soon she could paddle on one side and the boat still went almost straight.

There's nothing to it, she thought as she reached the middle of the river. And then she saw the fin.

It was dark and ominous, cutting through the water. Zarah's heart leaped into her throat. Her hands froze on the paddle. She had seen the *Jaws* movies. She had seen shark programs on TV. Sharks could rip a boat like this one into pieces with their sharp teeth. They thought everything dark was a seal. They chewed up divers in black wet suits all the time, mistaking them for seals. They didn't like human meat but couldn't tell the difference.

"I'm human," Zarah shouted at the shark. Maybe her orange gloves would save her. Seals don't have orange hands. She hoped the shark realized that.

The shark rolled into a deep dive. It came up on the other side of the boat, then flipped into the air. Sharks didn't do that. "You're a porpoise." Zarah almost laughed with relief. Quanamina had said that porpoises were a sign of good luck when they came up in the river from the ocean.

The boat's belly scraped on the soft mud of the other side of the river. The tide didn't seem to be turning yet. Junior had whizzed them across to Barnett in about five minutes. She didn't know how much time she had before the tide changed. But she could always step out into the marsh and pull the boat along. If she had to. She might sink up to her chin in the seething, clicking marsh mud. Zarah breathed in its rich dark smell.

There were fiddler crabs on this side already running around in the mud, clacking their claws at her. Zarah shuddered. She was wearing tennis shoes but they could still bite her ankles if she put her feet in that mud, soft as jelly.

A crocodilian log in the marsh made her heart leap again. But it didn't move and when she got closer she saw that it really was a log with two turtles—kutas—sunning themselves on top. She pushed the boat through the mud, half poling, half paddling. The mud made sucking sounds when the paddle went too deep.

The green blur of Barnett grew larger until Zarah could see individual trees, the dock, and even the store behind the dock. She didn't see any people. It was too early or perhaps too late. People who went out to fish usually went before dawn the way Junior did.

Zarah paddled across the channel that separated Barnett from the marsh. The tide was turning now. She could see little ripples on the surface of the water. She shoved the boat onto the shore and tied it to a tree instead of the dock. Zarah preferred the solid feel of the land beneath the bow of the boat when she got out of it. She took off the gloves and left them in the boat. This was the easy part.

The store was open when Zarah approached but she still didn't see any people. She didn't go inside. A dog lay across the doorway. He was busy chewing his paw and didn't even look up as she went into the phone booth. She pulled a quarter and the lawyer's card out of her pocket.

But first she dialed her number in New York. If Ila were there she would accept the collect call.

"The number you have reached is not in service," came the operator's pinched voice.

Zarah dialed Londra's number. She would be asleep if she were home. Zarah let it ring for a long time but there was no answer. She had tried. Now there was nothing to do but go through with her plan.

She dialed the number Shelby James Cosgrove had written on the card. "This is my home phone number," he'd said. "Tell your grandmother to call me anytime, day or night, if she changes her mind." After three rings a woman's sleepy voice answered.

Zarah took a deep breath and pretended she was doing an exercise for acting class. "Can I speak to Mr. Cosgrove?" she said in a little girl's voice.

"It's for you," the woman said. "I don't know who."

There was a bump, then the lawyer said, "Shelby Cosgrove here."

Zarah swallowed. "Mr. Cosgrove, my grandmother ask me to call. She ready to sell."

"Who is this? Who is your grandmother?"

"This Sarah Jane Brown. My grandmother, she Quanamina Brown."

There was a silence. Then he said, "What does she want?"

"She say she ready to sell. But she say you got to come right now and bring cash money."

"I can't come right now. I don't have the money here."

This was the important part. He had to come now. She couldn't hide the fact of Quanamina's death for long. Not in the humid heat of Domingo. "She say you come in a hour. She might change her mind."

"My god, Flora, she's come through," Zarah heard him say. "This could mean millions!" His words were muffled, as though he had his hand over the mouthpiece of the telephone.

Then he spoke directly into the receiver. "I don't know if I can be there in an hour," he began.

"She say you come alone and bring cash money. In a hour." Zarah hung the phone up. The receiver was wet where her hand had sweated on it. She wiped both hands on the seat of her shorts and ran down to the boat.

The tide had turned now and was beginning to race in the direction of Domingo. All she had to do was ride it back and steer the boat over to the bank. It was much easier than the trip over.

FIFTEEN

~~~~~~~~

LOOMIS had finished sweeping around the house when Zarah got back from Barnett. He was sitting on the back steps with the frizzle chicken in his lap, singing the alphabet song to it softly.

"I'm back, Loomis." The chicken jumped out of his lap and flew off the steps. Loomis stood up and smiled but the worry lines were still on his forehead. She would have to get him out of the way while the lawyer was here.

"How would you like to catch us a mess of crabs? We'll surprise Quanamina."

She sent him to the river with a crab line. "You stay out of the water now, Loomis," she told him, "and wait there until I come for you."

She went to her room, walking quietly across the floor. She didn't know why she was being quiet. There was no one to hear her now.

The hated white dress hung in the back of the chifforobe.

Zarah took it out and looked at it. She remembered Quanamina's gnarled hands heating the iron on the cookstove, smoothing the dress on the ironing board. The dress still had the imprint of Quanamina's iron. But now it was too fresh for her purposes. She had to disguise herself so Shelby Cosgrove wouldn't realize how old she was. She didn't want him to suspect anything. He wouldn't recognize her from before if she presented herself as a little girl.

But he wouldn't expect a little girl in a clean starched dress in the middle of the morning either. She balled up the white dress and rubbed dust on it to make it look like she'd been playing outside. She felt as though she were dirtying Quanamina but it had to be done. She pulled the dress over her head and buttoned it, but she left the sash untied. Little girls' sashes were always coming untied. She put her hair in little girl braids and tied them with some red yarn she found in the sewing box. She checked herself in the mirror. She thought she looked about ten, maybe younger, twelve tops. She kicked her sneakers off. She would have to chance worms and bites.

In the living room she sat down with the will and copied Quanamina's signature. It wasn't hard. Her grandmother had barely been able to write her name. Zarah didn't think she had ever been to school. Maybe Quanamina's father had taught her to write her name. She couldn't read much, even with her glasses. She had held the Bible on her lap for comfort or to look at the pictures. She must have memorized all those verses from listening to the preacher all her life.

After a few tries Zarah thought nobody could ever tell the difference between her signature and Quanamina's. She put the will back in the Bible and she went outside to wait for Mr. Cosgrove. She wished she had a doll. She wanted to look innocent and naive and shy so he would never suspect anything.

He came about two hours after her phone call, sweating as he hurried along the sandy shell road. He was wearing pink trousers and a pink tie with a fishing lure embroidered on it. He had a briefcase in one hand and a small square suitcase in the other.

Zarah met him under a tree where she had dragged a porch chair. She stood up and looked down at the ground as she said, "She say you wait out here. She feeling poorly." She hoped she sounded like a native of South Carolina instead of New York. She drew in the dirt with her toe and peeped up at him through her lashes.

He didn't look pleased. "But I must see her so she can sign the papers."

"Nossir. She say it ain't fitten for a man to come in the house when she in bed." She knew he would do without a witness to the signing to get the land.

"This is highly irregular," he began.

"She say you wait here. She say we got to hurry because Mr. Saylor, he on the way here."

"In that case it would behoove us to hurry," he said quickly. Zarah watched him. He must know that Mr. Saylor would try to stop the sale.

"You got cash money?" she asked.

He opened the suitcase and showed her the money. He'd said he couldn't get it but she had known better. People like him knew how to get what they wanted.

He took some papers out of the briefcase. "This is the sale contract with the same terms as before with the house, cemetery, and right of way still hers. She will need to sign and date both copies and give me her deed to the property.

The buyer has already signed." He showed her the line to sign on.

Zarah took the contracts and went in the house, closing the door to the front porch behind her. She didn't want Shelby Cosgrove to see what she was about to do. She sat down in Quanamina's favorite green chair. "I have to do this, Quanamina," she whispered. "I hope you understand."

She copied her grandmother's name and then wrote the date the way she thought Quanamina would have written it on the two contracts. She took the deed out of Quanamina's Bible and put her copy of the contract in it. Then she went out on the porch.

Mr. Cosgrove was sitting in the chair fanning himself with his Panama hat. He stood up when he saw Zarah. She waved the papers at him to come closer.

"She say you put the money on the porch," she told him.

He started to say something but closed his lips and put the little suitcase inside the screen door. Zarah closed and latched it. Then she slid the papers under the door. She wasn't taking any chances on him getting the deed and refusing to give her the money.

He looked at the signature and seemed satisfied. Then he looked at Zarah "You one of her grandchildren?"

"Yessir, one of them."

"I think Mrs. Brown has done the right thing. Tell her I hope she will soon be feeling better."

"Yessir, I tell her."

He put his hat on and left. Zarah took the money to her room and checked it. It was all there. Money to get her and Loomis to New York and college and whatever else they needed for a long time. But for now she had to hide it. She wrapped the briefcase in several plastic bags and dug a shallow place in the cookshed. It would be safe there even if it rained. She put an empty crate over the spot.

～～～～～～～

LOOMIS had a basket full of crabs. "I got another one," he said when he saw her.

She sat beside him on the bank. "Loomis, I've got something to tell you. You know Quanamina has been feeling bad a lot lately."

He nodded. He had that scared look again.

"She was real sick during the night."

"Can the doctor fix her?"

"No, Loomis. She died."

His eyes filled up and tears spilled down his cheeks. He stood holding the crab line, crying silently in the soft summer morning. Zarah felt tears in her eyes, too. She put her arms around him and he hugged her, sobbing now. She held him for a long time.

When he was quiet she said, "I've got to tell somebody about Quanamina. When is Junior coming?"

He sucked in his breath. "Soon."

"Let's go wait for him."

"What about the crabs?"

"Let them go." She watched as he tipped the basket into the river. The crabs sank to the bottom like stones.

She held his hand as they walked to the landing to wait for Junior.

SIXTEEN

~~~~~~~~~~

WHERE Sister Brown's burial dress?" Sister Beale asked Zarah.

Zarah thought fast. Quanamina had intended the white piqué for her burial dress. Her only good dress was the shabby pink one she had worn to church. Zarah didn't want her grandmother buried in that. She went to the trunk in the sitting room and opened it. The orchid peignoir lay in the same folds that Quanamina had handed it back to Zarah to put in the trunk that first night, disturbed only when her grandmother had taken out the white piqué.

"Here it is," she said.

"Oh, let me see." Sister Monroe hurried into the room from the kitchen where she was supervising the food people had sent over from Barnett.

Zarah shook the peignoir free of its folds. The sweet herbs fell on the floor leaving their tingly sweet-sharp smell in the air. For a moment Zarah could see Quanamina as she had been that first night, her swollen fingers stroking the soft peignoir.

"That sure is a pretty color," Sister Monroe started to say, then she broke off and peered through her glasses. "That not a dress."

"It a nightgown," Sister Beale said. Her lips tightened with disapproval. "It won't do. Sister Brown got to be buried in a dress."

"No," Zarah said. "This is a peignoir, not a nightgown. A hostess gown," she improvised. "Quanamina loved it. She wanted to be buried in it."

Quanamina hadn't said so but Zarah knew she was right. She had seen it in the way Quanamina had touched the peignoir. She had kept it in the chest for special things, the white piqué. Quanamina had loved pretty things. She hadn't had many in her life. Zarah wanted her grandmother to rest through eternity in a beautiful gown. Besides, there wasn't anything else. Zarah refused to bury her grandmother in the shabby pink church dress.

"This funeral be a scandal," Sister Beale said.

If she only knew all the scandal that had happened that day, Zarah thought.

When Junior had come with the milk Zarah had told him about Quanamina. He had known what to do. He had gone back to Barnett and brought over Sister Beale and Sister Monroe to run the funeral. The lodge would take care of everything, including expenses, they told Zarah. They had bustled in, tying flowered bib aprons over their black church dresses and taken charge—Sister Beale the funeral, Sister Monroe the kitchen. They were experts, Junior had assured Zarah.

The doctor came from Beaufort and said that Quanamina

had died from a heart attack in her sleep. Dr. Toomer was a dark, small man with a wrinkled face. In his black suit, he looked like a symbol for death itself, Zarah thought. He patted Zarah's hand and told her that Quanamina didn't suffer. She knew that from her grandmother's facial expression. But it was comforting to hear it from a doctor.

"The funeral must be today in this heat," he told Sister Beale. "I bet it's already 95° in the shade."

"We got to have the setting up," she said, shaking her head. Her gray curls swayed.

"Without embalming, you have to have the burial today," Dr. Toomer said.

"It all got to be done proper," Sister Beale argued. "If it not, Sister Brown soul won't rest. It walk around forever."

"You can do it all proper," Dr. Toomer said, irritably, "but do it all today." He threw up his hands. "I don't want to hear anymore. You can have the setting up and funeral by nightfall. Make sure it is done," he said to Junior. "I'll check back later."

Others from the church brought food, the same dishes that had been at the church dinner. Zarah was tired and wanted to sleep but not with the house full of people. She wasn't hungry but Loomis needed to eat so she fixed herself a plate and one for him. They ate on the back porch, throwing tidbits to the frizzle chicken. It scrambled for each bite as though it had never eaten before. Zarah felt as though she hadn't either. The glass of milk she had drunk that morning, the trip to Barnett seemed to have happened long ago.

Junior and four other men came out on the porch. "They want you to come in now," he said. He and the men took shovels they had left propped against the cookshed and went down the path to the graveyard.

"Stay here with Frizzle," Zarah told Loomis.

The women had cleared the sitting room, shoving the furniture into Quanamina's bedroom. A wooden box had been set up on sawhorses. At first Zarah thought the box was filled with flowers. Then she realized that it was Quanamina in her orchid peignoir lying in her coffin.

The coffin was encircled by women from the church. They were humming in a low mournful rhythm and sobbing. It was the saddest sound Zarah had ever heard. It seemed to seep into her skin and her heart and she realized that Quanamina was dead forever. But looking at the serene expression on Quanamina's face she felt at the same time that it wasn't so bad, that it was a kind of natural thing like telling time by the tides and the seasons.

Zarah called Loomis and took him into her room and helped him get dressed in his suit.

"What they doing?" he asked as she tied his tie.

"They're singing for Quanamina," she said. She didn't know how to explain a funeral to Loomis. She wasn't sure herself what they were doing. "It's like a sort of going-away party," she told him. "Sometimes, when people leave, their friends have a party to wish them a safe and speedy trip. That's what they're doing for Quanamina."

"Where she going?"

Zarah didn't answer for a minute. Finally she said, "To a better place." But she wasn't sure that Quanamina had believed that, not the way she had loved Domingo.

"Wait out on the porch," she told him.

Zarah opened the chifforobe and looked through the dresses she had brought. The only black dress was crushed velvet and cut too low for a funeral. The other dresses were party dresses. The white piqué was dirty but she wouldn't have worn it anyway. She pulled out the purple Charmeuse. It would have to do. She remembered reading somewhere that purple was a mourning color.

She fluffed up her hair until it was a black cloud over her head. Then she tied a purple paisley scarf across her forehead in a headband and slipped in Navajo earrings that swung like full silver moons above her shoulders. She would go to the funeral in style.

Sister Beale was waiting for her in the hall. "Humph," she said. "I knew you'd wear something else scandalous. You disrespecting your grandmother."

"I don't disrespect my grandmother. I don't have a suitable black dress. Anyway, in some countries, purple is a mourning color."

Sister Monroe stuck her head in the door from the other room. "Not here. We wear black to funerals."

"My mother and I wore blue to my father's funeral. I hope people will wear red and yellow and green to my funeral or any color that makes them feel good." She went out on the porch to find Loomis. She didn't want to cause a scandal at Quanamina's funeral but she had to stand up for herself.

By 3:30 Reverend Zeke had arrived and the house and yard were filled with people from Barnett. The moaning and keening had been nonstop and Zarah's nerves were on edge.

She pulled Junior aside and asked how much longer before the funeral.

"It's already started," he said. He was wearing his church clothes. He and seven other men nailed the lid on the coffin. Sister Beale covered the top with pink roses and the men lifted it on their shoulders. The circle of mourners moved along with the coffin as it was borne down the steps and along the path to the graveyard. Zarah walked behind it holding Loomis's hand and trying not to turn her ankle on the uneven path. At least her pumps were black if her dress was not. But they weren't made for walking on uneven dirt paths. The earrings bounced gaudily against her neck. There was no need for them. With her free hand Zarah slipped the earrings out of her ears and into the pocket of her dress.

The graveyard was somber under the cedars. The shade seemed heavy. Zarah felt it leaning on the back of her neck. The grave Junior had dug was a dark hole, waiting to be filled. Reverend Ezekiel stood at the head. Loomis's fingers tightened in Zarah's hand. She squeezed them twice.

"Jesus said unto her, I am the resurrection and the life: he that believeth in me, though he were dead, yet shall he live.

"And whosoever believeth in me shall never die. Believeth thou this?"

"Yea, Lord," the mourners answered.

Zarah's heels sank into the soft sand. She breathed in the cool aromatic cedar smell. A breeze drove the gnats and mosquitoes away. Zarah looked at the faces around her as the mourners intoned their dirge. It seemed that everybody from the church was there. She saw Lily and Bina and Ernestine with Ernestine's brothers. She smiled at them but they didn't smile back. Everybody looked serious and solemn.

And then they testified.

"Sister Brown was a child of the Lord."

"She walk the path of righteousness."

"The Lord was her shepherd."

"She walk with Jesus."

Finally Reverend Ezekiel ended with the Twenty-third Psalm. "The Lord is my shepherd, I shall not want." he recited. Junior and the pallbearers slowly lowered the coffin into the grave with ropes. The ropes rasped as they were pulled from underneath the coffin. Sister Beale handed a clod of dirt to Zarah and one to Loomis. Zarah squeezed the clod until it became soft and sandy in her hand, then she leaned over and dropped it into the grave.

"Put yours in, too," she said to Loomis.

He let the dirt drop from his fingers. It fell on the ground beside his feet. A few grains went over the edge into the grave. That was good enough, Zarah thought. It was all symbolic anyway. It couldn't really cushion the weight of the grave filling the way the minister had said it would at her father's funeral.

The men shoveled the sand into the grave. It sounded like a gentle rain sifting down on the roses.

Then Sister Beale poured a cup of black coffee into the sand and picked Loomis up. His mouth opened into a wide O but no sound came out as she held him out over the grave.

"What are you doing?" Zarah shouted, snatching Loomis away from her. He was shaking with fear as she pulled him close in a fierce hug.

Sister Beale tried to drag him out of Zarah's arms but Zarah held on. She was stronger than Sister Beale.

"We got to pass him over the grave," Sister Beale explained. "The youngest child got to be pass over the grave."

"No! You can't do that."

"We got to," Sister Beale said.

"No. He's afraid." She could feel his heart beating fast against her knee where he crouched against her. "He'll have nightmares forever."

"If we don't, the spirit won't rest. It have to walk the island forever." Sister Beale shook her finger in front of Zarah's face.

"No," Zarah said again. "Quanamina would rather walk the island forever than to scare Loomis. She would have died herself to protect Loomis."

Everyone was looking at her as she picked Loomis up. But no one made a move to stop her as she carried him back to the house. He was crying as she locked the door to her room and sat him on her bed. "It's OK, Loomis. You're safe now. I won't let them do anything to you."

He looked up at her with sad, tearful eyes. "But Quanamina gone be a hant."

"No, she won't. If she walks this island, it will be because she loves it too much to leave. You know how she loved Domingo, Loomis."

He nodded. He was still sniffling as she blew his nose on a piece of tissue she found in her purse. She had caused a scandal at Quanamina's funeral but this time she knew that Quanamina would approve.

SEVENTEEN

~~~~~~

ZARAH folded the purple dress and laid it on top of the others. She wouldn't need them for awhile. Besides, she had clothes in New York. She shook out the white church dress. She had to pack it dirty. There had been no time to wash it but she could do it later. She refolded the dress and put it in the box. Quanamina's love was in that dress, in every stitch she'd made with her gnarled arthritic hands. Zarah closed the box and sealed it with the tape Junior had brought when he delivered the packing box. He'd promised to mail it for her if she left it on the screened porch.

Loomis watched from the glider. He had hardly let her out of his sight since the funeral. He'd slept on a pallet in her room and followed her around all morning as she packed the box and her suitcases.

After the funeral the mourners had all left before sunset,

including Sister Beale and Sister Monroe. They both went muttering dire predictions about Quanamina's spirit but Zarah wasn't afraid. Quanamina's spirit would not do anything to frighten Loomis.

Reverend Zeke, Lily, Junior and his wife, Dorothy, had stayed until after dark. They'd wanted to take Loomis and Zarah over to Barnett to stay with Lily's family. But Zarah had refused. "We have to go back to New York tomorrow," she'd said. They had to get away before anybody found out about the sale. "But we will come back and visit you maybe next summer."

Dr. Toomer came back and had a plate of food with them. "Sister Beale runs a good funeral," he'd said, "but she gets carried away sometimes. I didn't know she was still doing that passing over business at funerals. I'll have a talk with her."

Reverend Zeke had smiled and said, "I wish you luck. Sister Beale is powerfully forceful. Powerfully forceful."

Dr. Toomer had looked at Zarah then and said. "Maybe we better keep you here to rescue little children from Sister Beale at funerals."

"I'll let Lily take over for me. She rescues animals," Zarah had replied. "Just think of the kids as animals," she had said to Lily.

Lily had smiled at that. "I'll try."

Zarah wrote her address on the top of the box. "There, it's all ready to go to New York."

"I don't know how to cook," Loomis said suddenly.

"Well, of course you don't. Nobody does at five."

"How I gone eat?"

"What do you mean?"

"I be all by myself if you leave."

Zarah sat back on her heels. "Loomis, you don't think I'm going to leave you here alone, do you?"

He nodded.

"I'm going to take you to New York with me. I thought you knew that."

He shook his head. "I didn't know that."

"We're going to ride all the way to New York City on a bus but we won't get there until tomorrow. I'll tell you what. You go and pick out what you want to take with you. I have some things to do. When I come back we will pack your things in my suitcase. OK?"

The worry lines on his forehead melted away and he almost smiled. "OK." He jumped off the glider making it thump against the house wall as he ran to find his things.

Zarah picked up her Walkman and went to the cemetery. Quanamina's grave next to Henry's was mounded with loose sand. A large funeral wreath of pink roses stood at the head of the grave. A card was tucked into the center. Zarah pulled it out and read it. William and Eleanor Saylor. The coffee cup Sister Beale had emptied lay upside down on the top of the grave. A bowl and spoon lay beside it. Not much to help her in the afterlife, Zarah thought.

A whispery breeze ran through the cedars. They seemed almost to breathe and Zarah could almost believe in ghosts, almost believe that the people buried here were watching her. Counting on her. The cement slabs of the graves blurred into the pale sand as Zarah's eyes teared. "I'll make it," she told them. "Loomis and I are going to make it."

She popped Ila's gospel tape, the one Quanamina had liked best, into the Walkman and turned the sound low, low enough for a spirit to hear it but too low for a passerby, and laid it beneath the wreath.

"I'm walking, walking, walking in the spirit of the Lord," came Ila's voice. Zarah felt a strong need to see her mother, to hug her, to hear her gospels and blues and silly songs around the house. Ila was much more like her sister than her mother. Now she would have to be Loomis's mother-sister.

She left the Walkman playing low. The tape would play until it or the battery wore out or until the first rain. It would play Quanamina into the next world. Or it would play for her if she stayed on Domingo.

The tide was coming in as Zarah reached the beach. She took off her sneakers and walked barefoot in the sand one last time. At the stream she went over the low dunes and stood listening to the sounds of the island, the seething singing woods on her right, the sighing of the ocean on the left. Light fell through the trees, dappling the stream yellow, brown, with patches of green where weeds grew along the bottom. The water ran in lazy ripples past bulrushes, between a cleft in the dunes, cutting a wide shallow trough in the sand until it disappeared in the ocean. A stick no more than a foot from her right toe suddenly slid over the dry leaves on the bank into the stream. It swam against the ripples like a blade of long dark grass until it disappeared into the darkness of the upstream swamp.

And then her mind registered the fact that she had just seen a snake. A snake. She had seen a snake. It hadn't bitten her or chased her or flashed its fangs at her or even threatened her. It had only gone its own way doing its own thing. The snake was a natural part of Domingo.

It belonged here to the woods, the stream, the swamp.

Zarah crossed the stream, passed the *barre* tree. There was no time for a workout today. When she came to the shell road she put her sneakers on. She followed the shell road to the Saylors' and rang the front doorbell.

Mrs. Saylor answered. If she was surprised to see Zarah, she didn't show it. "Come in," she said. "Benicia went to Charleston this morning." She took Zarah through the wide hall to the living room. "Sit down," she invited. "Would you like some lemonade?"

"No, thank you."

"I am so sorry about Quanamina. We didn't come to the funeral. We didn't know if you would have wanted us. We knew her all our lives. I grew up here, you know. My husband and I are cousins."

"I didn't know."

"Yes. I was an orphan. My parents were lost in a storm at sea. I came to the island, a scared child of seven and have been here ever since." She gave a little laugh. "I think Quanamina and I both believe that these islands are paradise."

Zarah smiled. "Yes, Quanamina thought that."

"And now Domingo is yours. I hope you will think it is paradise, too."

Zarah decided not to tell her that Domingo had been sold. She was sure to demand an investigation. She could never prove anything but she might cause a lot of trouble for Zarah and Loomis.

"It is the most beautiful place I've ever seen," she said. "Could I have Benicia's address in California? I'm taking Loomis to New York and I won't have a chance to see her before we go. She said she's going back next week."

"Yes, she is supposed to go then. We'd hoped that she

would stay longer with us." She rose and crossed the wide hall into the study. Zarah heard her open a desk.

The living room was soft peach, yellow, and pale green. From the ornate ceiling molding to the wide polished pine boards with the four-inch thick pastel flowered rugs, the room made Zarah feel serene. The tall windows with their wavy glass were bright with leaf-filtered light. The surfaces were dotted with just enough light to make the room glow but never glare. Zarah thought that the builders of this house had planned all of this. It was not accidental. They knew how to create this harmony.

Zarah wondered how they could reconcile this beauty with the evil that made it possible, slavery, how they could compartmentalize their minds so that they could enjoy their lives of ease while others toiled and died to produce it. She didn't understand people who could create such beauty and at the same time allow slavery. A snatch of one of Ila's songs came into her head.

> When you climb
> that magic hill,
> and life's mysteries
> are revealed,
> what then, my friend,
> what then?

Mrs. Saylor came back with a swish of her dark blue skirt and handed Zarah a card. Zarah stood up and put the card in the pocket of her shorts.

"I'm sure Benicia will be so sorry she missed you," Mrs. Saylor said.

"Yes. I am, too." She trailed behind Mrs. Saylor, her fingertips touching the gleaming surface of a mahogany table, the curve of a silver bowl, the raised pattern of a porcelain vase, leaving her fingerprints behind.

~~~~~~~~~~

HEY, wait up!"

Benicia caught up with her at the beach. "I just got back," she panted. "I was afraid I'd missed you. Are you really going back to New York today?"

Zarah nodded. "School will be starting. I've got a million things to do. Loomis is going back with me. I've got to find a kindergarten for him and buy him some clothes and teach him about New York. I don't think he's ever been off these three islands, Domingo, Saylor, and Barnett."

"I guess it will be like another planet to him," Benicia said.

"Yeah. But he learns fast." He'd had Quanamina's fierce protective love for the first five years of his life the way Zarah had had her father's for almost seven. Now he had her and Ila and Londra. He would be all right.

"I'm sorry about your grandmother. It must have been a shock."

"It was. She had been sick but she seemed so tough, as though she would live forever." Zarah realized that it had been a shock to discover how she felt about her grandmother but there hadn't been time to think about it then. She'd had too much to do.

They stood on the damp sand and watched the ocean. The waves lifted in the blue-green water, rising and furling until they reached a foaming crescendo and rushing onto the beach. Then they slid back quietly, leaving a lacy trail on the sand until the next wave flowed over it and left its own lacy trail for a few seconds.

"Will you write to me?" Benicia asked.

"I got your address already."

"Give me yours."

"I don't have a pen."

"Write it in the sand and I'll come back and copy it."

"Better do it before the tide comes in," Zarah said as she scratched her address in the sand with a piece of shell.

"Maybe you could come to California sometime. Loomis, too."

"That would be fun. And you have to come to New York."

"You can finish teaching me that dance from *The Nutcracker*." Suddenly Benicia ran around the beach with her head down.

"What are you doing?" Zarah asked. "Are you having a fit?"

"I'm looking for something."

"What?"

"Something. Oh, these will do." She stooped down and picked up something in the sand, then held out her hand. Two bits of shell lay on her palm. They looked as though they had been carved deliberately instead of accidentally by worms and waves. The shell pieces were the color of dark honey and each had a tiny hole in it.

"We can wear them on a thong or a chain to remind us of our summer here."

Zarah closed her fist around the shell bit. "I won't ever forget," she said.

EIGHTEEN

~~~~~~~

ZARAH wrapped the money in two pillowcases until it made a smooth mound. She put the mound in the middle of another pillowcase and tied the two ends around her waist. Then she slipped Quanamina's pink dress over her head. She was tall, five and a half feet last time she was measured at the ballet school. The dress was long enough but even with the pillow, it billowed around her. That was good. It made her seem really pregnant.

She had kept out enough of the money in her purse to buy their bus tickets to New York and some for emergencies. But she had decided to play a pregnant woman on the trip in order to hide the money. Now no one would be able to rob her. No one would ever guess that she had money hidden.

She put on her sneakers and closed the big suitcase. Loomis had had few things to put in it. He'd outgrown most of his clothes or they were unsuitable for New York. His only toys were the worn teddy bear his mother had sent him once and the ball she'd found on the beach. Zarah checked the house for anything she might have forgotten. Then she gathered their things and locked the front door. She left the key in the flowerpot in case Junior needed to get in.

The big suitcase was lighter this time as she and Loomis walked down the shell road. It didn't bounce the way it had before. She had folded the shoulder bag and put it in the big one. She had left the Bloomingdale's bag behind. Most of her things were packed in the box to be shipped. She had only brought her jewelry, her tapes, one dress, and Loomis's bear. The biggest thing in the suitcase was the family Bible. She had wanted to mail it because it was so heavy but then she thought if it were lost, she could never replace it. The Bible was their link to Quanamina and the past now. They were leaving Domingo but Zarah thought it was also going with them, that it was part of her just as her daddy's death, her first experience with ballet, Ila's songs, Londra's friendship, and all the sad and happy things in her life were. Domingo was in her bones, her blood, her brain.

They had almost reached the plank bridge when Loomis said, "What about the chickens?"

"I gave them to Junior. He is coming for them as soon as he builds a pen."

"But what about Frizzle?"

"We won't need him in New York. He's going to live with Lily."

"Are there conjure bags in New York?"

"No, Loomis. And no hu hus either except in the zoo where people go on Sundays to see the animals. They have bears and lions and tigers there, too."

"They have elephants?"

"Yes. And seals and zebras."

"I heard of elephants."

"You'll hear of lots of other things from now on, Loomis." Zarah planned to teach him nursery rhymes and tell him fairy tales all the way to New York. By the time they got there, he would have them all memorized.

They crossed the plank bridge. The tide was going out. Someday the marsh that separated the two islands might silt up and the two would be one island again. A great blue heron was fishing in the marsh. It stared at them as they passed, then returned to its task.

The shell road on Saylor's Island was thicker than the one on Domingo. The suitcase didn't roll as well. Once it fell over. Zarah righted it.

"It's already tired," Zarah joked.

"It don't want to go," Loomis said.

Zarah took his hand. "It has to go, Loomis. It's time for it to go. That's its job, to go when it's time to."

They paused at the top of the camel bridge. The Culebra River snaked its way around islands, marshes, on its way to the sea. This would be their last look at Domingo, Saylor, and Barnett for a long time. They could come back someday. But the island would never be the same again. Zarah didn't want to say this to Loomis. Instead, she said, "Don't ever forget this world, Loomis." She spread her arms.

"I won't." His eyes were dark, absorbing the islands, the marshes. She knew he wouldn't and neither would she. It was their past, their heritage, Quanamina, slavery, the island, the marshes. But now it was time to move on.

"Look, there's a boat. Is it Junior?" she asked. But the boat was too far away to tell. They both waved anyway.

The bus came along soon after they reached the highway. Zarah bought tickets to Charleston. They would have to change there. As she heaved the suitcase into the aisle, she saw two white women looking at her. "Look at that," one of them said. "She can't be more than fifteen."

"She's after that welfare money," the other one said. "It's a crying shame. Somebody ought to put a stop to it."

"She must be older than that. She has one kid already."

Zarah smiled to herself. Her disguise was working. She rubbed her back, the way she had seen pregnant women do. She found two seats on the ocean side of the bus and fanned herself with her ticket. "It sho hot today," she said in a loud voice. "I be glad when I ain't carrying around so much."

The women frowned and looked away. They would clack about her all the way to Charleston. Zarah felt the way she did when she had learned a new dance sequence.

Zarah had packed a lunch in one of the baskets Quanamina had woven. She put it on the floor. "We'll have a bite later," she said to Loomis, "when we feel more like eating."

She took off Quanamina's hat and put it in the overhead. The pink roses bobbed over the edge with the movement of the bus. Loomis stared out the window.

"Where's Domingo?" he asked.

"Yonder," she said, pointing at the marsh behind them. "Yonder lies Domingo."

Brenda Seabrooke was born in Mt. Dora, Florida, and grew up in Fitzgerald, Georgia, the setting for her highly acclaimed *Judy Scuppernong*. "As far back as I can remember," she says, "about the age of three, I wanted to be a writer. I thought books were magic. Writing them had to be even more magical."

Brenda Seabrooke was graduated from Newcomb College in New Orleans. She is married to a retired Coast Guard officer, and they have lived around the edges of the United States. The parents of two grown children, she and her husband now live in West Virginia, along with a houseful of animals.